TROUBLE IN TAHOE

PRAISE FOR WES RAND

"The unconventional collected works of Wes Rand was recommended to me. I can say these are not for the whimsical as you'll wish that only bandits, outlaws, and wildlife, are the only things to fear. Bring a gun as you sit down to read and pray you are not on the wrong side of Major Neville Stryker."

— **DIANE KAWASAKI**, WRITER AND STAR OF
TLC'S HIT SHOW MY LITTLE LIFE

"Gritty, dark, and fast-paced—If you love frontier action, Wes Rand's EVIL STRYKER SERIES will knock you out of the saddle."

— *ERIC J. GUIGNARD*, AWARD-WINNING AUTHOR,
AND EDITOR, INCLUDING *AFTER DEATH...* AND
BAGGAGE OF ETERNAL NIGHT, BRAM STOKER
AWARD-WINNER

"As a filmmaker, I can see the vibrant images come to life on every page as Evil Stryker crosses every line of decency and yet leaves the women wanting him and the men wanting to be him. Wes has created an anti-hero of devastating impact."

— **VINCENT ROCCA**, WRITER/DIRECTOR OF
KISSES AND CAROMS, AUTHOR OF *11 SIMPLE STEPS
TO TURN A SCREENPLAY INTO A MARKETABLE
MOVIE: OR, HOW I GOT A $10K MOVIE TO GROSS $1
MILLION THROUGH WARNER BROS*

"A wild ride through the old west, filled with unforgettable characters and plenty of action. This series hits all the marks! You're going to love Evil Stryker!"

— **JOHN PALISANO,** VICE PRESIDENT OF THE *HORROR WRITERS ASSOCIATION* AND BRAM STOKER AWARD-WINNING AUTHOR OF *NIGHT OF 1,000 BEASTS*

"Evil Stryker operates like a confident, skilled executioner across its violent Western landscape."

— **DALLAS SONNIER**, PRODUCER OF BONE TOMAHAWK

ALSO BY WES RAND

Left to Die - Book 1

Cross Cut - Book 2

Payback is Hell - Book 3

To Die For - Book 4

The Christmas Slay - Book 5

TROUBLE IN TAHOE

Book VI in the Evil Stryker Series

WES RAND

TROUBLE IN TAHOE-

BOOK VI IN THE EVIL STRYKER SERIES

Copyright © 2022 by Wes Rand

Cover Copyright © 2022 by Wes Rand

Published by Wild West Books

All Rights Reserved.

Cover Illustration by Linda Nilsen Worker
lindanilsenworker.com

Editing Services and Formatting: Stacey Smekofske EditsByStacey.com

ISBN Paperback: 978-1-7362400-8-3

ISBN ePub: 978-1-7362400-9-0

Printed in the United States of America.

No part of this book may be used or reproduced in any manner whatsoever without written permission from the author except in the case of brief quotations embodied in critical articles or reviews. This is a work of fiction, no resemblance to persons living or dead was intended by the author. Thank you for supporting art.

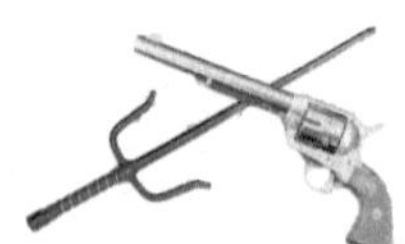

For Doctor Quynh Feikes

No matter how well you do what you do, there will always be some asshole who'll come along to tell you you're no good at it.

CHAPTER ONE

Major Neville Stryker rode early out of Pescadero on the tall roan horse. Fog rolled in from the sea a mile away, and he allowed the horse to take its time to the beach trail. He was in no hurry. When he arrived, he would make his most difficult decision of the day, whether to ride up the coast or down the coast, and he'd decide that when he saw the waves rolling in.

"I don't know nothing 'bout him." Elena answered. When asked, she always answered with that response. The strong Mexican lady ran the boarding house. "He gets on that big horse an' rides out to the beach every mornin'. If'n you wanna know more, ask him yourself."

No one in the sleepy little town asks him anything. Stryker's appearance does not invite conversation. He is a tall man, six feet-three inches, and lean, he tips the scales at two hundred pounds. He's part Mexican, Asian, and Scandinavian and the mixed breed couldn't care less where he comes from. His black hair hangs long and straight, and with a few gray strands it stretches to the shoulders. He wears his mustache Mexican style, drooping at the ends under a hawk billed nose. A week-old beard runs along his jawline. His face is tan and weathered, due to long stints in the western sun. Crow's feet radiated from his pale gray eyes which closely resemble a raptor's. The lines on his face are not laugh lines.

Above sharp cheek bones and beneath ridged brows, his ghostly eyes fling icy daggers, even when he isn't in a killing mood. He is a man best left alone.

"There was a killing a few months ago, a woman and her two boys. A fellow said he saw someone that looked a lot like your boarder riding the trail where they found the bodies. What do ya think about that?" A wiry little man and his little wiry wife were both around forty something years old. They stood at the front door since they hadn't been invited in.

Elena had never liked them. They were busy bodies; she knew the type. They were the kind who liked to run around, wanting to be the first to spread gossip and hoping to get a surprised and embarrassed reaction. Some people live for it. These two did. The man fidgeted with a worn hat he held in his hands, and he talked fast with the irritating dialect of a smart ass. The woman nodded as if her husband spouted honest to God truths. Busy bodies. You had to wonder if their sex was shitty, and this was how they got off. *Was spreading gossip as good for you as it was for me?*

"When he returns, I'll bring him over to your house. You can ask him about it. Still living in your mama's old house north of town, Phillip?" Elena smiled sweetly.

Phillip threw on his hat. "Uh, no. That's okay," he said. "C'mon, Millie." He grabbed his wife's arm and took off, dragging her down the street. Millie hopped with quick little running steps to keep up with him.

Elena watched them for a bit and then closed the door. She returned to the kitchen. Her lone boarder liked steak and eggs for breakfast. She sat the coffee pot on the wood stove to boil. He liked his morning brew strong and black, and she expected him back from his ride in a half hour. Although he carried no watch, the man was uncannily punctual. He wasn't fussy, but she could tell it pleased him if he found breakfast on the table when he walked through the door. And for some reason, she never tried to understand. She wanted to please him.

Elena didn't know it, but Stryker had killed the two boys and their mother. Their ambush hadn't gone well.

Ruthless killer, words aptly used to describe Stryker. The winding trail of the past twenty or so years led him to Pescadero. It lay peppered with violence and tragic losses–his life had a lot of scar tissue. Those events honed his skills, but they also shaped him, causing him to sometimes act like a cornered animal, vicious and snarling. He was dangerous to cross.

He had no friends. Two people in San Francisco could've been called friends by some: George Hearst, a US Senator, and the female mining engineer who worked for Hearst, a widow named Morgan Bickford. But neither one was a friend. He sometimes went on secret missions for the senator. He sometimes sampled the charms of the woman.

His enemies occupy graves. Those he knew about anyway. No one got a second chance, not even a good-looking mother of two boys. They'd tried to kill him. Robbery was their motive. Isolated and by himself while camping on the trail late at night, he might have seemed like easy prey. He wasn't.

Years of use and harsh weather had worn off some of the stamped letters on his saddle skirt–MAJOR NEVILLE STRYKER. Many people thought what remained was a better fit–EVIL STRYKER.

The two-mile ride to the coast from Pescadero took twenty minutes. The morning fog had burned off, and the sun warmed his back. A few white puffy clouds hung in the bright blue sky. In the distance, he saw another rider on the sandy trail, ambling down the coast from the north. When Stryker got to the beach, he stopped to take in all that was with the sea. Waves rolled in and crashed, making peals of thunder before exhausting themselves and running up the sand. Sea gulls squawked overhead. Seals and sea lions barked at each other on small rocky islands in the water. Kelp floated lazily on the swells, and there was the distinctive smell of the ocean, briny, moist, and heavy. Brisk and fresh mornings were the best. There was something special about watching the sea awaken. Stryker's days here began calm and peaceful. He turned south.

The beach trail ran along the grassy edge of the thirty-foot escarpment above the water. Tall grass and ice plants carpeted the gentle slopes, rising from the beach cliffs up to hills blanketed with pines. A few miles down the coast, the tower of Pigeon Point Lighthouse came into view. Stryker pulled the roan off the trail about a half mile north of the navigational station and dismounted. He wanted a solitary ride. The lighthouse, or the small house at its base, was sometimes staffed even during daylight hours. The hills gave birth to a ravine that deepened as it sloped lower and cut through the cliff. It allowed access to the beach via a footpath, winding down thru the gully. He'd stopped here often. He even made a crude bench from a wooden plank that washed up on the sand below. It sat on two rocks he'd hauled from the agate rock spit at the cliff's bottom; the bench was good for sitting and watching. The grass lay trampled and worn in front of the plank; he wasn't the only person to use the bench. He pulled the bridle off the roan and replaced it with a rope halter from his saddlebag. He didn't stake or tie off the rope. Letting the end drag along the ground was enough to keep the big horse from wandering too far.

Stryker was not a man given to idle dreaming, and he didn't use the time by the sea to reflect. His life was filled with violence and killings. It began its bloody saga when he witnessed his parents butchered in front of him when he was a boy. Union thugs on the Embarcadero beat and stabbed them to death. A few years later, young Stryker killed two bullies, sons of the union men. He'd been trained to defend himself by his mother's half brother, an Asian master in martial arts. Neville's mother, part Asian, part Scandinavian, and his father, part Mexican and whoever had stimulated his grandfather's loins on one particular day, made Stryker akin to a mongrel dog. Not that Stryker cared. He lived. One day he would not. And religion? He and God left each other alone.

His uncle sent him east to save his life. There he got caught up in the Civil War and eventually graduated from West Point Military Academy. He later fought in Indian campaigns and remained in the Army until he met the girl he would marry, Leigh. She and her family died during an artillery demonstration gone wrong when a munitions competitor switched firing coordinates on the howitzers. That man's murder made Stryker a wanted fugitive.

He was good with a gun and handy with a razor, but it was the weapon his uncle taught him to fight with that chilled a man's spine. The sinister-looking sai was normally used in pairs. Originally, one was used as a farming tool, then two were modified to defend against the Samurai sword. It had a long center tine flanked by two shorter ones. Stryker carried only a single sai with tines sharpened to needle points, hanging in a pouch by the small of his back. Two would have been uncomfortable, and one was all he needed. More than one dying man marveled at the weapon as his blood dripped from the tines.

As Stryker sat on the wooden plank, he didn't think of the past: the men he'd killed, or the women he'd known. He didn't think of his dead wife. He had none of the maddening nightmares of Leigh while he sat on the bench. Maybe that's why he liked to linger by the sea. Instead, he watched a sailing ship on the horizon, wondering where it came from and where it was going.

He'd been sitting on the bench a good twenty minutes when he again noticed the lone rider on the trail coming his way. Although he sat relaxed, he continued to scan around him. A soldier's habit. The person was a quarter mile away. He watched the rider, half of him anyway, because a rise in the land shielded the man's lower half and all the horse. Then the horse crested the mound, and the full man came into view along with the dapple-gray horse he rode. Stryker thought the rider's shape seemed a little too diminutive to be a man. Then he realized the rider was a she.

Stryker continued to scan 360 degrees, not focusing on the woman, but he let his squinty eyes pause on her with each round of surveillance. She reined in ten feet from him. The gray splayed its hind legs and peed.

Hello, Stryker. Remember me? Reba?[1]"

Stryker remembered the girl, but he said nothing.

Reba swung off the gray and led it to the bench. The top two buttons on her shirt were unbuttoned, displaying tempting cleavage. She wore very tight denims. If she farted, she'd probably blow off a riding boot, and when she bent to loop the reins on the plank, Stryker noticed the girl had a good saddle seat as well. She appeared older than her early twenty-something years. Pretty, but Stryker figured the girl had peered under the hood of manhood more than a few times. She had the look. You know the kind that said she liked grinding it out. If he were of the religion that wanted 72 virgins in paradise, he'd rather have 72 sluts, and Reba could be one of those. She had sharp cheekbones and was kind of thin in the face, with full lips and mischievous green eyes. He might even have twin Reba's. *Yep, girls like her could really fuck up a man. I better wait for paradise.*

She scooted down beside him on the bench, playfully bumping his hip with hers. "Hello, Stryker."

He moved over to make more room.

"Elena said you ride out here every day."

"I like time alone," he said without a smile. He'd known girls like Reba before. Trouble, that's what they were. Maybe she'd been teasing those boys who tried to rape her. Girls like her come on to a kid, flirt, and jerk him around, maybe dangle him on a string and laugh while doing it. He didn't understand their kind. He didn't like the Reba's in the world, and he stayed away from them. He'd try hard not to smack her.

"Well, I didn't exactly follow you. Besides, I wouldn't know where you go when you get out here." Reba pointed at the distant lighthouse. "I work there."

"You do." He didn't bother to speculate what a person would do at a lighthouse during the day.

She must have guessed he might have wondered though because she answered his unspoken question. "I clean the tower and the house once a week. Men are pigs. The State pays me." Reba leaned to the side and picked a magenta bloom from an ice plant. "Why are you here?"

"Exercising the horse." Stryker said.

"No, I mean in Pescadero. Inquiring minds, there's talk."

"Talk." *You're probably the one doing the talking.*

"Yep, talk. Some say you might'a had something to do with the killin' of the Hoskins woman and her boys. It happened a few months ago."

Stryker ignored her, but she neared the edge. He squinted at the ship. It sailed parallel to land about a mile offshore, heading north. Maybe it was heading for San Francisco.

"You know, I don't think I properly thanked you for saving me from a raping, maybe a killin' too.[2]" Reba turned to him as she spoke. "And just so you know, they never did find them boy's bodies. They washed out with the tide like I said they would. Never showed up. Sharks got 'em, I guess. I'm grateful you came along that day, Stryker." She sounded sincere.

He looked at the girl. She was studying his face, seemingly waiting for some kind of acknowledgment. He nodded and turned back to the ship.

"I was in Frank's Bar," she began innocently. She swung her gaze to the far-away ship with Stryker. "I heard 'em. It was a man and wife, I mean. And I don't like them two. Anyway, they were saying someone who looked a lot like you was ridin' the same trail the night the mother and her boys got killed."

Stryker stared out at the glimmering sea and said nothing.

"Even though I saw how good you are at shootin' I knew you couldn't a done it."

Stryker canted his head toward her.

"I told 'em so, too. You was with me that night, all night. You left after I cooked you breakfast the next morning. That's what I told everybody, all right." Reba turned to Stryker. "You suppose that makes us square, Stryker?"

"Reckon so, Reba." He watched her get up and climb back on the horse. He watched her ride toward the lighthouse, and he watched her disappear after she crested a rise and rode down the other side.

The ship became a distant dot as it continued north. It would soon be totally out of sight. Stryker rose, removed the roan's halter, and put on the bridle. He swung into the saddle and let the big horse keep its own pace back to Pescadero. *Shit, could've been wrong about that girl.*

Elena had his breakfast ready. "You hungry this morning, Mister Stryker?" She smiled warmly. Elena was a middle-aged widow; she and Stryker got along well. "I have the *Examiner* for you. It's on the table. Sit down." She handed him a cup of steaming black coffee. "Read your paper, and I'll bring your breakfast out in a minute."

The crumpled newspaper normally took a few days to reach Pescadero. Regardless, Stryker wanted to read it. Besides learning about old news, he had another reason to get the *Examiner*. Before he read the news, he checked the personals. That's where he usually found a notice from San Francisco, telling him about a new job for Senator Hearst. But what he really looked for was a message from the woman, Morgan Bickford. He might have asked her to marry him if it weren't for the memories and nightmares about Leigh–and the damned jinx. The jinx killed every woman who came near him. At one time, he thought Morgan had been killed, too. Stryker wasn't superstitious or religious. All he knew was that he existed, and one day he would not. But even the most rational of men, the most pragmatic, will react irrationally if every time he does a certain thing he gets knocked down. It seemed as if a permanent mate was forbidden. Why and by, whom or what, he had no idea. He told himself it made little sense. It was a foolish notion. Still, it happened time after time. All the women died. Over the years, their graves hammered the reality of the jinx into him. Now, he couldn't chance it. He would never again extend his hand to a woman. If he stayed far enough away, maybe Morgan would live. A mining engineer, she resided in San Francisco when not out inspecting the mines for Hearst. He'd stay in Pescadero.

Elena brought him breakfast prior to his reading all the *personals*. The savory aroma of steak with eggs fried sunny side up slathered in butter persuaded Stryker to lay the *Examiner* on the table. She left the kitchen, knowing Stryker liked to eat and read the paper alone. Thirty minutes later, he finished the meal and the second cup of coffee. He picked up the paper again and saw the short personal:

To NS. Please come to S.F. In need of your services. MB.

He sat the paper aside and lifted the cup. Realizing it was empty, he placed it back on the table. Pensively, he spun the cup. *Wouldn't want to admit it, but lately I've felt in need of her services too.* Of course, he knew that wasn't what Morgan meant. He raised the cup an inch, clanked it on the wooden table as if a decision was made, and got to his feet.

"Elena."

The woman quickly appeared. Stryker wondered if she'd been at the door ease-dropping on his thoughts.

"You want more eggs? Coffee?" Elena swept past Stryker and grabbed the Meyers coffee pot off the stove.

He knew she knew. The routine–he'd read something in the Examiner's personal section and disappear for weeks or months. "No."

Elena sat the pot back on the stove. "You goin' away, Mister Stryker?" Elena couldn't read well. She never tried to find what prompted him to leave town, and she never asked why.

He nodded.

"Well, Mister Stryker. You take care." Elena stood by the stove. She flinched her arms twice as if there was something she wanted to do, but her nerve failed both times. She gave up and abruptly spun away, hurriedly leaving the kitchen.

Stryker stared at the door behind her, picked up his cup, and stepped over to the stove, where he poured himself half a cup.

CHAPTER TWO

An hour later, Stryker was on the dirt road to San Jose. Once there, he'd load the roan on the *Central Pacific* and ride the train to San Francisco. A routine–these undertakings for Senator Hearst had become recurring jobs, dangerous and deadly. A while back, Hearst had sent the United States Cavalry to save Styrker's life and paid him an enormous amount of money to procure ownership of the *Examiner* for Randolph, the senator's son. Stryker owed the man. How many more times would he pay on the debt? He hadn't done the math. Besides, he'd see Morgan. She would never replace his dead wife, but he liked and admired her. He liked her a lot. Something about the damn woman attracted him. Yeah, she was good-looking, but it was more than that. She expressed principles and values that made a man feel free and noble.

It was a two-day ride to San Jose, and he'd broken camp an hour before sunup on the second day. Stryker's shadow faded as the sun settled lower on the Santa Cruz Mountains behind him. His butt and the roan were getting annoyed with each other as the town in the distance grew larger. Rain started as he reached the San Jose station. It wasn't heavy, but it was enough to where a man who had good sense would get out of it.

"Train's not coming in today," the ticket manager in the window booth said. The balding man wore a billed cap, and he continued scribbling on chits of paper while he spoke. He didn't look up. "They're replacing sections of narrow gauge with standard rails this week. Be rollin' next week if you can wait. Got two stages running. Got room on that one. It's leavin' when filled." He pointed at the stagecoach parked at the north end of the station platform with his pencil. "Two dollars."

Rain fell harder, making the decision easy. Stryker threw two silver coins against the man's chest.

The ticket manager slammed the pencil down in anger and jerked up his head. Once he saw the mixed breed's fierce features, nothing came out his gaping mouth. He shoved a ticket through the window, picked up the pencil, and went back to his scribbling.

The stagecoach waited empty of drivers in the pelting rain. The two drivers, being of good sense, stood around the corner under an eave, smoking their cigarettes. They eyed Stryker with apprehension as the tall man headed to the coach. If he boarded, they would have to take the driver's seats. They flicked their smokes and stepped out into the rain.

Stryker took the bridle from the roan and put on a halter. After tying the horse to the rear of the stagecoach, he grabbed the Winchester and climbed inside. The cushions, seat backs, and walls of the Wells Fargo Concorde were black padded leather. At least it had that going for it, but the nostrils had to adjust to the dust and musky odor. Railroads were making stagecoaches obsolete, and this one had been out of use for a few years. The route ran on the old Butterfield trail on the west side of the San Francisco Bay.

Four people already waited in the coach: a man, his wife, and their two children, who sat across from them. Mail bags on the floor served as footrests. Two expensive pieces of luggage sat between the children. Stryker figured a seat had been bought for the luggage to keep it off the roof rack and out of the rain.

"Come over here, children." The pretty young woman in a powder blue dress patted the cushion between her and her husband. The man sported a brown suit with a purple bowtie. The boy and girl leaped from the seat where they'd been sitting and hopped across the mail bags. The stage line hadn't cleaned the seats, and their damp clothing turned from dust to mud on children's rumps. The parents scooted farther apart and made room for the boy and girl to sit between them. The mother flashed Stryker a nervous smile, which disappeared after he took off the leather duster, spraying water on her and the kids.

"Name's Chester," the husband stated. He was a handsome man, appearing to be in his midthirties, and a suitable match for the attractive wife. "This is my wife Chloe, my twin children Charlie and Candice. They're six." The twins wore matching color and design outfits. They stared blankly at Stryker. Although he was five-foot-ten and trim, Chester still had to sit at an angle to make room for his wife and their two children. He eyed the extra space by Stryker with conspicuous envy.

The "C"s family was too cute for Stryker. He declined to offer a seat on his side of the coach. He found such familial penchants for matching names, clothing, or activities annoying. He glanced at Chloe and then back at Chester.

"Stryker." He folded the coat and laid it on top of the luggage. Outside, one driver yelled a command, and the stagecoach lurched forward. Interrupted by the coach's loud creaks, squeaks, and groans talking stopped. Stryker dipped the Stetson over his brow and stretched out his legs.

The boy and his sister sat uncomfortably scrunched between their parents, busying themselves with elbow jabs. The attractive mother with curly blond hair, rosy cheeks, and dazzling blue eyes retained ten pounds of a long-ago pregnancy. She busied herself fidgeting in her train case. After a more than moderate jab and the resulting "ow," she tapped her son's arm and shook her head. The twins then sat quietly and stared at Stryker. They launched into their best behavior, perhaps thinking it best not to annoy the mean-looking man who stretched out his legs under their dangling feet.

Ten miles up the San Jose Road to San Francisco, Chester read a newspaper while his wife and twins dozed. Stagecoach rocking tended to make passengers nauseous or sleepy. However, it seemed as if Chester wanted to keep a watchful eye on the none-too-friendly man across from him. He remained awake. He finished reading and then tossed the paper on the mail bags piled on the floor.

Stryker shoved the Stetson's brim up with a forefinger. His pale eyes locked onto Chester's.

"Are you going all the way to San Francisco?" Chester asked. Stryker's hard stare made him uneasy.

"Yes."

"I see." Chester straightened and peered outside. "Looks like the rain's letting up. You have business there?" He turned back to Stryker.

"Yes."

Chester glanced at his snoozing family and smiled. "I'm taking them to the theater tomorrow, and then sailing the following day. It'll be the first time in San Francisco for the twins. We live in San Jose. I'm a doctor there." He paused for a comment from Stryker, which never came. He offered another smile and asked good-naturedly, "And where might you be from, sir?"

This time, Stryker hesitated. He leaned out the window and looked up at the dwindling rain. "Hell."

Outside, the stagecoach slowed. The boy seated next to Chester woke, rubbed his eyes, and asked, "We're stopping father?"

Stryker watched them, wondering who taught children of well-to-do families to use "father."

"Yes, Charlie. We have to change horses. We need to get fresh ones every ten or twelve miles. Long trips are completed in stages." Chester looked at Stryker, using a knowing smile at this teachable moment. "That's why they're called stagecoaches."

The stage rolled to a stop in front of the small Spanish-styled waystation. Eighty-foot eucalyptus trees surrounded the building. Planted during the gold rush years ago, they were part of the state's effort to beautify the bay area with trees from Australia. With the little picturesque station nestled in among the tall trees and resting on tall California Field Sedge grass, an artist would have done well to put the idyllic setting on canvas.

Stryker reached for the coach door, but it swung open before he could grasp the handle. The ten-year lad opening the door set a footstool on the ground. Stryker, already leaning forward, swung out and went to the roan. He untied the horse and led it to the water trough. After allowing the horse to suck water, he brought it to the side of the building. He got a handful of oats from the saddlebag and threw them on the grass. While the big horse ate, Stryker brushed off the dust and mud. He groomed the roan and decided to ride it the rest of the way to San Francisco. The perfect family in the coach was getting on his nerves. He'd give them a head start before starting out. The roan needed a rest, anyway. He went into the station to wait.

The Spartan ten-by-ten front room had two bare circular tables with chairs. In back was a small kitchen. Normally, the station would provide breakfast or at least coffee to the passengers, but it was empty of culinary help. Trains did not need to stop at the station, and while work was being made on the rails, the line only provided horse exchanges for the stagecoach. He came back outside, sat against a eucalyptus tree, and watched the stagecoach roll away. One driver glanced his way but didn't call out they were leaving.

"I'm glad that man didn't get back on," Chloe said a few minutes after they'd pulled away from the station. "I've never seen a man who looked so vile."

"Now, dear. I don't think he meant us harm."

"Those eyes. If death had eyes, they'd look like his." Chloe shuddered, adding "Oooh, my God, he gave me the jeebies."

"Father, what does 'jeebies' mean?" Charlie asked, tugging on Chester's sleeve.

"Something your mother made up. Nervous, I guess. That man who was on the coach made her nervous." Chester made an obvious effort to change the mood by looking out the window and saying, "My, my, what a beautiful day."

"He gave me the jeebies too," said Candice.

Stryker rode out from the station an hour later. The trail wasn't as heavily traveled as when the Butterfield Stage used to run regularly. However, horse and wagon traffic kept the road clear of vegetation. It followed along the rails within sight of the San Francisco Bay, not a bad ride when it wasn't pouring down rain. A smattering of deciduous cottonwoods, sycamores, and walnut trees dotted the flat landscape. The giant redwoods grew farther west, closer to the coast where they got more rain in the Santa Cruz Mountains. He rode closer to the bay and searched for a suitable campsite near the water, and he failed to notice the wrecked stagecoach on the road a half mile ahead.

Ahead, closer to the road, he saw a dead, still upright cottonwood with broken branches laying on the surrounding ground. Good for firewood. Beyond that was the stagecoach on its side, and it took a moment for him to realize what he was seeing. He heeled the roan to approach the coach from the rear. It resembled a bloated dead cow with its wheels protruding like stiff legs.

Riding closer, he saw a body on the ground behind the stagecoach. It wore a powder blue dress. Near it, a coyote cautiously sniffed, perked his head up at Stryker, and trotted off. A hundred paces from the coach, Stryker dismounted and pulled the 44-40 from its scabbard and worked its lever. Scanning the surrounding area, he approached Chloe's body. He looped the roan's reins on the rear wheel and kneeled to examine her corpse. Her eyes were closed. The blood-stained dress was pushed up around her upper torso, and she was naked from the breasts down. Her legs lay spread apart, slightly bent at the knees. They were shapely legs, soft and smooth, and lifeless. Her face was bloodied, puffy, and badly bruised. She'd obviously put up a fight, but the welted bullet hole in her forehead meant she wouldn't remember the rape. He got to his feet and spied Chloe's undergarments laying ten feet away.

Stryker walked around the spoked wheels. Mail bags lay strewn on the ground, gutted down the middle with contents ripped out. Past the front of the stage, the driver's bodies lay on the ground on the far side of the coach. Stryker suspected they'd been shot on the driver's box, and were thrown to the ground when the coach overturned. A shotgun barrel poked out from under one of the men's chest. The horses were gone too, stolen along with whatever else was taken. He walked all the way around the overturned stage. The door remained slung open, and he stretched taller to peek inside. Chester lay on his back with his eyes open, suit jacket ripped open. A dark red splotch the size of a fry pan soiled his white shirt. Stryker heard a whimper and his eyes darted to the two small, huddled shapes in the corner.

"Shhhh," Charlie whispered, throwing his hand over Candice's mouth.

Stryker leaned in deeper. Squinting his eyes, he tried to see the kids better in the shadowed light.

Candice ripped her brother's hand away. "Don't hurt us!" she screamed. Charlie tried to cover her mouth again, but she shoved his hand away. "Please," she sobbed.

Stryker backed away from the door. Once again, he surveyed the surroundings. Seeing no one else alive or dead, he walked to the roan and shoved the 44-40 home. He gathered the reins and climbed into the saddle.

A half mile past the overturned stagecoach, Stryker came upon a black horse, maybe forty feet off the road, standing next to a eucalyptus tree. Getting closer, he then saw a man seated against its trunk.

Stryker reined the roan and did a 360 scan prior to riding closer. Ten paces from the tree, he pulled the Winchester and swung from the saddle.

The fellow was clean shaven, from what Stryker could tell. It became obvious why when he got closer. The boy wasn't old enough to grow facial hair. He was in his teens, and he had at least two or three years to go before he outgrew them. The boy's left shoulder, arm, and side were a bloody mess. So much so, Stryker wandered if the arm was still attached. There wasn't much life left in him, but he lifted his head upon hearing Stryker's spurs.

"I need a doctor." Getting no response from the mixed breed, he mumbled, "Was on stage there." He tried to lift his good arm and point. "Hold up. Chased 'em an' they shot me. Gotta help me to a doctor."

Stryker fired the Winchester. The big 44-40 bullet blasted through the kid's head, splattering pieces of skull and brains on the tree trunk behind him. Stryker hadn't seen him board the stagecoach, and he'd been wounded by a shotgun. Good enough. He climbed back on the roan and sat for a long moment staring at the man's horse. It was all black except a white star on its forehead; the stallion was a magnificent beauty. Saddle and bridle, black as well and tooled with the finest leather. The dead kid had one hell of a horse and saddle.

Those kids back there. They brought back dark memories. He recalled when his own parents were butchered in front of him. He'd been seven years old.

Men burst through the front door. Thugs dressed in black and wearing ladies' stockings on their heads, they'd come from the Embarcadero, the wharf by San Francisco, five or six of them. Rushing in swinging knives and blackjacks, they slashed and bludgeoned his mother and father. He'd sat on the floor and watched his mother bleed to death.

His Asian uncle took Neville in, but boys in school and especially those boys along the wharf bullied him. His mother was part Asian, part Mexican, his father was Northern European, which meant he didn't look like the others, and the grievances the boy's fathers had with his parents carried over to their sons who bullied and beat young Neville. One day, one night actually, that stopped. Neville's uncle was an immigrated Shaolin Monk, a master in the martial art of Kung Fu. His uncle taught him in secret. It took years of training, strict discipline, and patience, but Neville learned to fight, to kill. Then one rainy night when he was fourteen, he caught a bully in the alley and killed him. Killed him with the sai, then he killed another. His uncle rightfully reasoned Neville planned to kill them all and sent his nephew east to continue his schooling.

Those kids back there. Someone will come along and rescue them. Some old motherly type, a gentle father, a good man like his uncle, will take them in. *They'll be fine,* he tried to rationalize. *But maybe not. What if they're assholes? I couldn't give a shit.*

Stryker studied the dead man's horse, a prize for sure, but that's not why he stared at it. *That cursed thing caused all this damn thinking, remembering. Giving me ideas, I ought to shoot the fucking horse. What's it doing out here? Why didn't the other robbers take it with them? That kid by the tree couldn't have used it.*

"Ah, fuck." Stryker leaned down and grabbed the black's reins. "You kids, come outta there," he said, peering into the coach. He saw them in the fading light, huddled close together deep in the corner, but they were not moving and not responding.

"I'll shoot you if you don't come out." Stryker paused, then said, "You're coming with me, dammit."

"C'mon, Candy." Charlie struggled to his feet. He grasped his sister's arm and reached his hand up to Stryker. Stryker pulled the children up the floor, which was now a wall and managed to get them out of the coach. At one point Candice had to brace a foot against her dead father, but she was too afraid of the man pulling them out to squeal.

Stryker threw Charlie on the black. "Scoot up to the saddle horn. Make room for your sister."

Charlie turned to watch Candice get lifted and placed behind him. As he did, he saw his mother's body on the ground back of the stage. "Mister, what about our mother?" Tears welled up in his eyes.

"Your folks are dead." Stryker picked up the reins and led the horse and the new orphans to the roan. He swung into the saddle. "Hold on to your brother, Candice."

It would be dark soon, but Stryker wanted to put distance between them and the stagecoach. He figured the kids had gotten little sleep, and he had to keep looking over his shoulder to make sure they remained awake. They'd been through quite an ordeal, maybe even a degree of shock. Their father was shot and killed next to them; their mother was dragged out of the coach and raped. They surely heard her cries. They surely heard the gunshot that silenced them.

Shelter of some kind would be welcomed; however, if he found none in the next hour, he'd pull over by some of the live oak shrub trees and throw a lean-to together. An hour later, that's what he did. A small brook ran through the trees. Good enough. He made Charlie and Candice gather kindling while he tended to the horses. He pulled off the bedrolls and started the fire. The wood was wet. Stryker retrieved his hatchet and with pine-pitch sticks from his saddlebag, and he got the fire going. It smoked and sputtered before it took hold. He gathered more dead branches and told the kids to keep the fire fed while he looked for bigger limbs on the ground.

He sharpened two five-foot tree limbs, and then, using the back of the hatchet, he drove them in the ground five feet apart. He cut another limb and used more of the rope to secure it to the tops of upright poles. Next, he angled four more sharpened limbs in the ground and lashed their other ends to the horizontal pole with a leather string. Then he layered six-foot tree limbs up the diagonal poles. He'd left enough rope on the uprights to weave down the layered limbs. When finished, the lean-to was fastened together without having to cut his rope. He cut small leafy branches and placed them on the lean-to with the leaves pointed toward the ground. He'd untie the rope and leather in the morning. Gathering and preparing the tree limbs took most of the time. Once he got them cut, he'd built the lean-to in fifteen minutes.

The crude shelter was built within a few feet of the campfire so that the flames would provide reflective heat inside. He tossed in both bed rolls. The children could nestle completely under it with their feet pointed toward the fire. Stryker's upper torso would be under the shelter, not his long legs, though. He'd have to stretch them out beside the fire. *Good enough for now. Time to eat.*

"Sit there by the fire. Don't move," Stryker told the kids. The flames danced larger, throwing off more heat. Every so often, the fire would pop, sending glowing embers toward the stars before burning out. Charlie and Candice simply sat and stared at the fire. They saw the embers pop, but they didn't watch them rise.

Stryker left them to unsaddle the horses. He first led them to a nearby creek for water, then hobbled them in tall grass he figured would carry heavy dew in the morning. A quick study at the sky showed plenty of stars. You never know, though. He pulled the gear from the robber's horse and found a bag of flour and salted pork bacon wrapped in wax paper. In his own saddlebags, there were cooked beans, dried fruit, some hardtack, a small jar of oatmeal, and coffee. He hadn't planned on too many meals on the trail, especially meals shared with a couple of kids. If it hadn't been for Elena, he wouldn't even have had that. She'd worn a plain brown dress, a kerchief on her head and a sad smile the morning she gave him the vittles. The food sack was tied at the top with a string. He brought the sack, the robber's grub, and the canteens to the fire.

Charlie and Candice shivered by the fire. Stryker figured it was from the night chill, or maybe they were just scared. They sat together on the black saddle. Stryker sat on his. He poured water from a canteen into a tin cooking pot, then added beans and a piece of the bacon to make soup. Watery but at least it'd be something warm. When steam rose from the pot, he poured the contents into a clay bowl. He gave the bowl and a spoon to Candice.

"Eeoow! I don't like it." Candice hadn't tasted the soup. The bowl rested on her lap with the spoon submerged in the soup.

Stryker grabbed the bowl off her lap and gave it to Charlie. He glared at the boy, waiting for him to eat. The kid had five seconds. Charlie fished the spoon out in three, dipped it in the bowl, and gingerly, carefully, tasted the soup. He filled the spoon quicker on the next trip and slurped it clean. After several such trips, he filled the spoon halfway and offered it to his sister. She took it. She ate slowly, wearing an awful face. After that, Candice either liked the soup or just got used to it. She took the spoon from her brother and ate her fill. She dropped the spoon in the bowl and handed it back to Charlie. The boy ate a few more mouthfuls, peeked into the bowl, and gave it to Stryker. Stryker finished what was left and poured himself a cup of coffee. After finishing the coffee, he washed everything in the creek and returned to the fire.

"Mister Man," Candice began in a tiny wavering voice.

Stryker sipped the coffee. "Drink some water."

"When are you going to shoot us?" She didn't reach for a canteen.

"Shoot you," Stryker repeated.

"You said you were gonna shoot us," Charlie added.

"I'm puttin' it off for now."

Nothing was said for several minutes.

"If we help you get more firewood tomorrow and maybe do other stuff too, would you still have to shoot us?" Charlie asked.

"I'll think about it."

After they ate, Stryker rolled out the bedrolls. He laid one for the kids to lie on and covered them with the other. They had only worn light jackets. Stryker lay under his coat.

"Mister Man." Candice lay on her side, pressing her back against Charlie. "Where we going in the morning, if you don't shoot us?"

Stryker was on his back, arms folded across his chest, cursing himself because he went back for the kids. "San Francisco. You have relatives there?"

"No." Charlie propped up on one elbow behind his sister, looking over her shoulder. "We don't know anyone out here. Father brought us out from Richmond two months ago."

"Shit."

Stryker wasn't the consoling type. Perhaps that was best. If he'd thought about it, he might have theorized keeping the children frightened for their own lives kept grief at bay. Could be. Maybe they *were* too scared to grieve over their dead parents. So, he didn't hug or hold them, and he let them cry rivers. Another more caring person might do that later. And if it took a few days for that to happen—well, by then life will have inched forward. Yes, it could be that the cold heart of the mixed breed was the right medicine for now.

"Go to sleep. We're getting up early."

Stryker got up before sunrise and rebuilt the fire. He shook the coffee pot. It sloshed what sounded like a cup and he poured in more canteen water, leaving in the old grounds. After emptying the canteen into the cooking pot, he sat both pots on two sturdy parallel branches close to the flames. Carrying the empty canteens with him, he led the horses to the brook. Walking a few feet up-stream, he re-filled the canteens while the horses sucked from the creek. By the time he came back to camp, the morning grayed. The new day arrived with a heavy fog. As he saddled the roan and the black, he caught sight of Charlie and Candice crawling out of the lean-to. The boy said something to his sister and then the two of them went looking for firewood.

When Stryker came back to the fire, the children had made two trips with arms loaded with dead branches, but some of the wood was too rotten to burn.

"These are no good, too rotten." Stryker tossed them on the grass. "That's enough. Sit down." He poured oatmeal out of the jar into the steaming pot. The kids remained silent. Quiet, like they were waiting for something.

A few minutes later Stryker lifted the pot from the fire and sat it down, where he spooned hot oatmeal into the bowl used for soup the night before. Candice ate first without complaint, Charlie second, and Stryker last. The children sat quietly as Stryker finished his second cup of coffee.

"Kids, take the pots to the creek and wash 'em out. Use this soap." Stryker picked up the soap bar he'd used and threw it in the cook pot. "Fill them with water and come back to put out the fire. Make as many trips as you have to. I'll tear down the lean-to and saddle the horses."

Charlie and Candice jumped to their feet. Charlie grabbed the coffee pot. His sister lifted the wired handle of the cook pot, and they took off running.

"Come back here!" Stryker barked. The children walked back to Stryker. "Take the bowl and my cup." He handed the dishes to Charlie.

Stryker first untied the leather strips, undid the rope holding the poles together, and then snaked it out of the branches. He grabbed the bedrolls and saddle blankets and carried them to the horses. He put on their blankets, threw on the saddles, and secured the bedrolls behind them. He'd tightened both cinches and was adjusting the bridle on the roan when Carl and Candice came up behind him.

"Fire's out, Mister Man," Candice said.

Two men rode side by side, hardly talking. When they did, it was short, clipped gripes. They were in a bad mood.

"We shoulda' taken the fucking horse anyway," one groused.

"The kid…"

"The kid, shit. Shoulda' shot him, Maynard. Put him outta his misery." The fellow leaned to the side and hurled a glob of tobacco juice in anger.

"He's probably dead now, Josh."

"Yeah, and that fuckin' horse better be there."

"He'd a shot you. You know that. He weren't that bad then."

"Coulda snuck around him. Shit. I don't care how good he is, God-damnit." Josh spit again.

"What's the difference? You ain't gonna get to keep it, anyway."

"Bullshit. Ain't nobody takin' it away from me. Ain't nobody, you hear me, Maynard?"

"Listen, Josh. I heared somethin'."

The two men reined in.

"This fuckin' fog."

"Shhhh! I hear voices."

"Don't talk," Stryker ordered. "Get behind the lean-to. Do it now." The lean-to, with limbs and leaves still hanging in place, was about twenty paces away and the kids darted behind it. Stryker let go of the bridle. He stepped under the roan's neck and pulled the Winchester from its scabbard. Casually holding a hand in the repeater's lever and the barrel resting in the crook of his elbow, he appeared relaxed. That's how he appeared, anyway. He heard the men and horses before he saw them. Fog still hung heavy, and it was several more minutes before they came into view. They materialized out of the mist like ghostly apparitions a couple hundred feet away.

Josh spotted a tall man and the horses. Shapes in the fog. "There's a man and two horses, Maynard." They reined in, mumbled something to each other, and then goaded their mounts on toward the stranger.

"Morning," a gruff-looking man who appeared to be in his early forties grunted.

Stryker said nothing.

"Say, them's fine looking mounts you got there, mister," he continued. He had scraggly black hair, sprouting from under a heavily stained hat and a week-old beard that didn't quite hide his pockmarked face. With cold, hard eyes, he sat with his forearms resting on the saddle horn.

The other rider wore a longer beard, a brown one. He sat upright wearing a fake smile with his arm hanging down his right side and hand wrapped around the grip of a holstered .45.

"Mind if I asked where you got that black?" the first one asked. It was the kind of sneering question a smart ass would ask before starting a fight.

"Charleeee!" Candice whimpered from behind the wood.

Stryker heard it. It was the pitiful cry of a terrified child. Maybe she recognized the two men. Maybe she thought Stryker was gonna give her and Charlie to the two men.

Stryker swung the carbine from his elbow and fired. The .44 slug hit the second rider's chest, sending him rolling off the back of his horse. He broke his neck when he landed. Didn't matter he was dead before he hit the ground.

Stryker jacked another round.

The black-haired talker sat up. "Hold on, mister!" He lifted his arms in the air.

"How many ride with you?"

"Six."

Stryker shot him. The big caliber bullet smacked the center of Josh's forehead, flattening when it hit, and blowing a fist-sized chunk of skull out back of his head.

"I don't think they were friends, Candy," Charlie whispered to his sister.

Stryker pulled bridles off their horses and wrapped them around the saddle horns. The horses could follow them on their own or they could stay and graze until someone came along. "C'mon, you two," he shouted.

Charlie took Candice by the hand. They rose to their feet and came out from behind the lean-to.

Stryker lifted Charlie up first, then Candice. They started off with Stryker leading the black and the children. They stared at the two bodies as they rode past, but said nothing.

CHAPTER THREE

Stryker and the kids reached the town of Mayfield mid-afternoon. It was the next stage stop and a train station for the Central Pacific. Mayfield bordered the early township of Palo Alto (Spanish for a big stick and named after a tall redwood tree in town). The train ran from Mayfield on up to San Francisco and Stryker purchased three tickets. They had a two-hour wait, and Stryker brought them to an eatery some distance away, originally called Uncle Jim's Cabin.

Carl Otterson built the stage stop, inn, and dance hall in the 1850s and was recognized as the first commercial building in Palo Alto, but he'd sold it by the time Stryker and the children rode into Mayfield. A fellow named Valenti lived there, selling meats. It was a two-story wooden structure on what was then Lincoln Avenue (later changed to California Avenue). A large building for its day, it had a spacious first floor and around ten rooms for rent on the second level. Five square, upright posts supported a balcony running the width of the building's front. Stryker tied the horses outside, and they entered the butcher shop to wait for the train.

Inside, the shop was a deli with a sitting area, and he led the children to a small table with a painted-on checkerboard and two stacks of checkers. The saloon bar had been converted into a meat counter, with weight scales and canned jars of beef, duck, and chicken displayed along the top. A mirror still hung on the wall behind the counter. With no staff member around, Stryker left Charlie and Candice at the little table and strode over to stairs leading to the second floor. Two short sets of opposing stairs led to the first landing. From there, one long set rose to another landing, where two more flights curved to the second level. Rooms to let ringed around the four walls, leaving an open space in the center. The most coveted rooms faced the front with balconies over the boardwalk below.

A short, plump woman suddenly appeared at the far end of the counter. A swinging door to the kitchen hung behind a tall plate cabinet, and Stryker hadn't noticed the entrance. The big-titted waitress stopped brushing flour off her breasts when she saw Stryker. The children caught her eye as well.

"Ah, I didn't hear you come in." She spoke with a thick Italian accent.

"We're waiting for the train," Stryker said.

"Would you like to eat while you wait, you and your children?" She wiped her hands on the apron.

"Coffee. Black for me. Give them something, too." Stryker dipped the Stetson toward Charlie and Candice.

"I have coffee, yes. Milk and *cannoli* for the *piccini*." She smiled kindheartedly at the children. "You wait," she said. "I'll come back with the best *cannoli* you ever had." She wagged a finger, spun around, and marched back through the swinging door, perhaps wondering what two kids were doing with a man like Stryker. He didn't appear paternal.

"Mister Man?" Candice asked, in her diminutive, little-girl voice. "What are you going to do with us?"

Stryker stood by their table. *What am I going to do with them?* "Find someone to take care of you until your relatives are found."

"Sir," Charlie began, then paused a moment. "We don't know any relatives in California. We don't know any in Richmond either."

Stryker frowned at Charlie, then at Candice. She attempted a bashful smile, as if to say *sorry*.

"Jesus." Stryker was exasperated… and frustrated.

"Do you know him, Mister Man?" Candice asked.

"Uncles, aunts, cousins, you must know one of 'em." Stryker groused.

"Mother and Father met at an orphanage. Mother told us they met when they were children, just like we are," Charlie supplied.

"Christ." Stryker admired their grammar at such a young age. The parents were doing a good job–were, *but shit! Now what?*

"Sir, those two men you shot." Charlie tried to deepen his voice. "One of them shot Father. The other one was there too."

Stryker didn't ask which one killed their father. It didn't matter to him. One might have wondered if he killed the two men in retribution for murdering the parents, or because he wanted to keep the horse. However, if the truth be known, it was neither. They'd simply rubbed the mixed breed the wrong way.

"Tell me if you see another one."

"Yes, sir," Charlie replied in his best husky voice.

The squat–okay and short fat–waitress emerged from the kitchen holding a tray. She walked carefully across the wooden floor, taking short, measured steps, trying not to spill the milk or coffee.

"Here you are," she said cheerfully, placing the front half of the tray on the table. She set the milk and *cannoli* near the children and handed Stryker the coffee. Then she flipped the tray under her arm. "Thirty-five cents, mister." She held out an open palm to him.

"Coffee better be good," growled Stryker. He dug in a pocket and withdrew two coins. Instead of dropping them into her hand, he held the coins in an open palm for the woman to take.

The coffee was good, hot and hardy, and had a strong aroma. Stryker sipped it while he watched the children try to cut into the *cannoli.* Charlie finally gave up with the fork and picked his up to eat with his fingers. Candice copied her brother.

Outside, horse clops, animal snorts, and groaning saddle leather announced the arrival of new visitors. Men, at least two of them, mumbled a few gruff comments, too low to understand from inside. Stryker eased away from the children's table. He shifted the coffee mug to his left hand and turned toward the door. The men's boots thudded onto the boardwalk. Their spurs jangled noisily with every heavy step on the boards.

Two men came through the door. They stopped just inside, as if to position themselves for a quick exit. Both were muscular and stood over six feet. Their hands rested on top of their revolvers, still un-drawn. They let their eyes adjust to the darker confines as they surveyed the room. It didn't take long for their attention to settle on Stryker.

"That black horse outside, he yours?" The one asking moved to put himself between the door light and Stryker. The other man stepped farther in, distancing himself ten feet from his buddy. Not their first gun fight.

Nothing from the kids.

"He is now." Stryker's hand dropped to the butt of the Peacemaker.

"Who'd you buy him from?"

"Didn't buy 'im. Figured the man I killed wasn't gonna use him."

The man in the doorway stiffened. His gun hand twitched, but he made no move to draw. The brash boldness of the tall mixed breed might have provoked hesitation.

"That horse…"

"I killed the two men who came to get him."

"Duncan!" a man on the stairs called out."

Stryker didn't look to see who it was. He kept his eyes fixed on the man in the doorway, figuring if the fellow on the stairs was going to shoot, he would have already. From the corner of his eye, he could sense the man to the left of Duncan was holding off, too.

"He killed Josh, Maynard, and the kid!"

"And he'd kill you too. You're not fast enough–neither of you."

"I ain't so sure." Duncan flexed his fingers.

Stryker thought he might get the two in front, but not the man behind. He waited.

"Your kids, Stryker?"

Stryker fought to keep from turning around. *The man knew his name.*

"Their folks, killed on the stage."

"Duncan, I said, no killing!"

"The kid–Arizona, he brought it on." Duncan talked fast now. "The driver and the guard gave up, threw down their guns, and put their hands in the air. But Arizona saw the woman and pulled her out. Tried to have his way with her behind the stage, I reckon. She was yelling a lot. We heard a shot. The guard had another shotgun on the floor. He pulled it and shot Arizona when he came around. Then Josh shot the man inside the stage. Maynard killed the guard and the driver. What was we and Harris to do?"

"We, Duncan?"

A shot rang out behind Stryker.

Duncan suddenly jolted. Blood appeared on his chest–growing around a black bullet hole. He staggered out the door and collapsed.

Harris saw Duncan take the bullet and ran for the door. The second shot caught him between the shoulder blades, and he tripped over Duncan's body. He picked himself up, mounted his horse, and rode a mile out of town. Sometime during the mile, the man became a body, and then the body fell off the horse.

Stryker turned and faced the shooter. "Slade."

"Stryker."

"That should even the score." Slade[1], a dapper dresser in his stripped suit, descended the remaining stairs. "You could've killed me that day in Egalitaria. Why didn't you?"

"Out of bullets, I reckon." Actually, he wasn't. He thought Morgan was killed that day. Stryker hadn't killed Slade, a hired gun brought into the mining town of Bickford (renamed Egalitaria by a gang of Marxist thugs) to specifically kill the mixed breed. Slade was wounded, and Stryker chose not to finish him off. Professional courtesy? Hard to tell. Stryker is a complicated man.

"You wasn't outta bullets. You kids like them *cannoli*?" Slade brushed past Stryker and looked out the door. Duncan's body lay on the stoop and Harris was nowhere in sight. "He was coughing blood when he stumbled out the door. He ain't gonna last long," Slade mumbled, with his back to Stryker.

Charlie and Candice returned to munching on their pastries. No answer to Slade. They tried to be small, not in the picture.

"Slade!" Stryker called out.

Both children turned their eyes on Stryker, watching him calmly, seemingly inured to the violence. Charlie reached for his milk. He took a swallow, put the glass back on the table, and bit off another piece of *cannoli*. Candice bit into her *cannoli* too. A casual observer in the room might have found their behavior a bit odd.

Slade dropped low and spun. His gun hand flashed to his Colt, but Stryker had already drawn the Peacemaker. Slade relaxed his grip and straightened. "This it?"

"Put him on his horse." Stryker waved the gun barrel at Duncan's boots in the doorway. "Take the black and leave."

A hint of a smile crossed Slade's face. He nodded, turned, and stepped outside.

Stryker watched the kids eat their desserts, who seemingly paid no attention to Slade's grunting as he heaved the dead man on his horse outside. A few moments later, they heard rhythmic hoof clopping that soon faded away.

Stryker holstered the Peacemaker.

"I heard shots," the plump Italian said, pushing through the swing door.

"A man shot two snakes. They're gone now."

"You want more coffee?"

As Stryker extended the cup he still held, he studied the kids quietly sniffling and staring at the half-eaten *cannoli*. Shock was probably wearing off now. The deaths of their folks began to age. Grief was setting in, the lingering kind that never goes away, and would be hanging around like a reoccurring nightmare for the rest of their lives. Stryker held his cup in both hands, not drinking the coffee. *Shit.* And for the briefest of moments, the mean-ass killer felt a twinge of genuine pity. He pulled up a chair and sat with them to wait for the train. Not a single word was spoken until the train whistle sounded an hour and a half later. The Italian came out once more, walked halfway across the floor and stopped, turned around, and never came out again.

"Let's go." Stryker pushed from the table.

The children scooted from their chairs, leaving the rest of the uneaten cannoli on the plates. It might be noted here that for the rest of their long lives, Charlie and Candice never ate another *cannoli*. They trailed silently behind Stryker, leading the roan to the station. Stryker tied the horse to a rail and walked across the platform to the ticket booth. The kids followed closely now and stood on either side of him as he bought tickets for the three of them and the roan.

Stryker turned the roan over to the cattle car hand and the three of them walked to the edge of the platform and joined a group of twenty or so people waiting for the train. Several couples waited there as well, some older, some a lot older. Stryker counted six single men. At least they seemed to be traveling alone, and none wore a gun, none that he saw, and they all looked middle-aged. He also noticed three women travelers, a matronly looking older woman with a matronly looking younger woman, mother and daughter, maybe. The third woman was alone. She appeared to be in her late thirties or early forties, a schoolteacher type, with strands of gray in her hair, and she clutched a cloth satchel in front of her chest with both arms.

The Central Pacific train rolled around a curve a quarter mile away. The huge black engine crept toward them, belching angry bellows of steam. Then as it rumbled by, the thunderous monster shook the platform. It was at that moment something happened to Stryker which had never happened to him before.

Candice grabbed his hand, held it with both hers, and pressed against him. Charlie saw his sister's actions. Fright overwhelmed valor. He grabbed the other hand and held on with only one of his. He was braver. Sissies use two. If any of the other passengers suspected a kidnapping by the menacing mixed breed, their fears should have been assuaged by the children's reaction.

Stryker fought a strong impulse to jerk his hands away. *Shit. They haven't been on a train before.* So, he gripped back, but only a little. *Some hard-ass I am.*

The engine pulled ahead and stopped, aligning the coach cars in front of the platform. On up the line, the engine rested, blowing steam as if catching its breath before the next haul. Stryker pulled children with him toward one of the coaches and pushed his way toward the front of the other passengers. He lifted the kids onto the steps. "Back bench," he said once inside the coach.

Oak slat benches sat in rows down the coach, separated by a middle aisle. Each bench seated two adults or a grownup with two children. Benches arranged with backs pressed together, allowed seated passengers to face one another. Windows lining the walls provided light and air circulation. Charlie and Candice headed to the rear of the car and sat in the last seat, facing frontward. Stryker joined them, sitting near the aisle. The rest of the passengers filed in, filling the benches from front to back. Lagging last in line, the single female passenger came on. She walked down the aisle and took the last open bench across from Stryker and the children.

Seeing her from the front instead of the side as he'd seen earlier, she appeared different. Yeah, she still seemed past her prime, but the vestiges of attractiveness remained. Although, her gray hair pulled back and wrapped in a tight bun didn't help. Her facial features were sharp. If a man caressed her face, he might get cut. But the aquamarine blue eyes, *damn,* the orbs were deep enough to dive into. Unlike Stryker's, the crow's feet by her baby blues were probably grooved from a more friendly expression, and not from squinting in bright sunlight or behind a gun sight. The smile she gave Stryker and the children when she sat gave hints at that. Though brief, it lit up her face.

"Good day," she clipped. She glanced first at Stryker then at the children.

Stryker tipped the Stetson. The children only stared back.

He sat and studied the woman. She had a story, a past. *Why was she alone now?*

With so little response, she dug a thin book from her carry bag and opened it to read. She crossed her legs and rested her hands, holding the book on her leg.

The train jolted the couplings, causing the passengers to sway like grain in a field, and the view beyond the windows began to slowly scroll past. Occasionally, when the wind re-directed the engine smoke, it blew past the window and partially shielded the outdoor scenes. Open windows toward the front allowed some of the smoke in, and passengers could smell the acrid wafts. Regardless, open windows were tolerated. Some of the male passengers needed a bit of airing out.

Twenty minutes went by. Something the woman read must have tickled her funny bone. She giggled. She glanced up, embarrassed. "I'm sorry. I was reading about two children and their pet goat."

Stryker suspected something contrived. He'd thought it when she first withdrew a book too thin for an adult.

"Ma-am, is the goat named Billy?" Charlie asked.

"How did you know?" She put on a make-believe frown and then smiled.

"Is the book, *If You Give a Goat a Tin Can?*" Charlie asked.

"Why yes, it is!"

"Father used to read it to me and my sister. I liked the story. I learned to read it too."

"You can read?" Her surprise was genuine.

"We both can read," Candice asserted, nodding several times to buttress the claim.

Puzzled, the woman glanced at Stryker. "You're their father?"

"Their folks are dead." Stryker deadpanned.

"I'm so sorry." She looked at Charlie and then at Candice. "My goodness." She was thinking, doing the calculation. "Well, how long has it been since they passed away?" Once more, she looked at Stryker, scrunching her brow into a question.

"Yesterday."

"My God! Yesterday? How?" She asked, sitting up straight.

"Stagecoach robbery."

The children stared at the woman, letting the adults talk.

"Robbery. Did you have anything to do...?"

"Wasn't there. Have them sit with you. Read together, Miss...."

"Case... Carol. I'm Carol Case." Miss Case leaned forward and extended her hand to Stryker. "And yours, sir?" *More C's.* The handshake was formal and brief.

"Stryker," he replied, sitting back and pointing to the children. "He's Charlie, the girl is Candice."

"Please to meet you, Charlie, and Candice... and you too, Mister

Stryker." Carol laid the book on her lap and padded the bench on both sides of her. "Come sit and let's read together."

The kids scooted off the bench and sat with Miss Case. She held the book out so that sitting between Charlie and Candice; they could read along with her. And they did. The three of them sounded each word at the same time.

Outside, the train went around a curve and the engine could be seen ahead of the tender puffing smoke as it chugged along the tracks. Then behind them the livestock car and the faded red caboose trailed around the curve. However, neither Stryker, Miss Case, nor the children looked to see. Carol, Charlie, and Candice read while Stryker watched the woman interact with the kids.

"When Miss Case and the children finished reading, she said, "Your father taught you well. Was he a teacher?"

Candice shook her head.

"No, ma-am. He's a doctor." For the moment, Charlie forgot his father was dead.

"You must be very proud. Will you become a doctor like your father?"

"No. I want to be like him." Charlie pointed a stubby finger at Stryker.

Clearly confused, Miss Case eyed the mixed breed. She tried to appear unfazed, and failed. "That's very... uh... interesting. I... can't see... are you...?" She asked Stryker.

"I'm not a doctor," Stryker growled.

"Charlie, I'm... What is it that Mister Stryker does? I mean, that you would want to be like instead of your father?"

Charlie thought for a bit, then said, "When the bad men came and pulled mother out of the stagecoach, she yelled for my father to help her. Father stayed in the stagecoach."

"Then what happened?" Miss Case eyed Stryker looking both shocked and confused.

Stryker said nothing.

"The bad men killed mother," Charlie said, his voice trailing off. "Then they shot father, too."

"Oh, my God!" Miss Case exclaimed. Nothing was said for several minutes.

After a while, the woman collected herself and asked, "Tell me, Charlie, why you want to be like Mister Stryker?" She asked again, while smiling stiffly at Stryker.

"When the bad men came again this morning, Miss Case... Mister Man killed them." Charlie nodded emphatically. "They sat on their horses, and he shot them." Charlie made a gun with his hand. "Pow! Pow!"

Candice nodded. "I see." Miss Case paused pensively. She studied the killer. Hard to tell what she was thinking–perhaps it was concern over the boy's "shooting," or the impression Stryker made on the lad.

Stryker stared back impassively.

A few moments edged by, and she asked, "Mister Man, that's how they know you?" A hint of a smile appeared at the corner of her lips. "Shall I call you Mister Man too?"

"Stryker will do."

Miss Case turned to Charlie. "And you, child. Do go by Charles or Charlie?"

"Charlie, ma-am."

"Miss Case, I go by Candy," Candice offered.

"Charlie and Candy, I like those names."

"You're going to San Francisco," Stryker asked as a statement.

"Yes, yes, I am." Miss Case said with some hesitation. "And you Mister . . . Stryker, what do you plan to do?

"Why."

"Excuse me, why what?" Miss Case furrowed her brow, looking perplexed.

Charlie and Candy listened to the grown-ups. Candy shifted from one side of her butt to the other, straightening her skirt. Once satisfied, she settled back and folded her arms across her chest. Charlie fidgeted.

The steady cadence of 4-4-0 American-type steam locomotive filled the conversation's empty pause between Stryker and Miss Case. Other than two men seated toward the front having a friendly argument, the rest of the passengers had retreated into bored reticence.

"Why San Francisco," Stryker said. Again, not as a question.

"I'm looking for work. I lived in San Jose with my husband until last year. He died suddenly, and I need to support myself. I'm a teacher, been one for sixteen years. I think I'd like San Francisco better than San Jose, so I'll teach there. And you, Stryker, what line of work are you in?" She leaned forward as if genuinely interested.

"When we get to San Francisco, you'll go with me and these kids to meet a man."

"I will?" Miss Case stiffened, sat upright. "I think I have a say in what I'll do."

Stryker's steel grays narrowed. He wasn't smiling.

"No, I . . . is it with Charlie and Candy?"

"Yes."

"Well, I suppose I can spare a few minutes. What's it about?"

"A job."

Miss Case cocked her head. "Hmmm, what kind of job?"

"How did your husband die?" Stryker asked, actually saying it as a question.

"Mister Stryker, you can be quite vexing." Miss Case changed her mood. "Jeff usually kept a loaded gun by the door. He'd just checked it. I guess to make sure it was still loaded. When he set it down, he acciden-tally jammed the hammer on the door hinge, and it went off. That's what they said set it off. Shot him under the chin. Killed him. Now, what kind of job?"

It was clear Miss Case didn't like discussing her husband's death. Stryker wondered why. "We'll see when we meet him."

"Who? Meet who?" Curiosity, impatience, frustration, all of it showed on the woman's face.

"I have a meeting with him on another matter at the Palace Hotel. That's all you need to know now."

"The Palace?" The meeting being at the hotel must have quelled some of her apprehension. The Palace Hotel was one of the best hotels in the world at the time. She glanced first at Charlie, then Candy. Candy had fallen asleep. Charlie no longer fidgeted. A nap was creeping into him, too. "I do have my standards, if you know what I mean. I'll not engage in the unsavory, Mister Stryker."

"Depends on what's unsavory to you." Stryker lowered the brim of the Stetson.

The wheels clacked on monotonously, filling in where discussion left off. Even the pair of male arguers near the front must have settled the issue. Other passengers read something, looked out the window, or napped. Miss Case stared at the taciturn man seated across from her with his hat pulled down.

She tried to reason things out. The man with his shoulder length hair, faded denims, soiled Stetson, and weathered skin did not appear extraordinary. Yet, what few words he uttered were those of a learned man. She hadn't paid much attention earlier because of his fierce countenance. The eyes, they frightened her. Kids or no kids, she would have left him had he not said he was going to the Palace Hotel. *Who in God's name would he meet at the Palace?*

Miss Case hadn't been entirely truthful. She'd shot her husband.

[illegible] [illegible]

[illegible] [illegible] have been the [illegible]

[illegible] [illegible] [illegible] botanical [illegible]
[illegible] [illegible] techniques [illegible] with the
[illegible] [illegible] [illegible] [illegible]
[illegible] [illegible] [illegible] these two are still
are not all the same.

CHAPTER FOUR

Not much was said between Miss Case and Stryker for the rest of the trip to San Francisco. Not much was said between Miss Case and the children. She only had the one children's book in her carry bag. She'd found it searching for another book to read on the train. It was a book she'd meant to read to her first-grade class that morning—that day, the day she never got to school. She stood and allowed the children to sit together at the window. They sat quietly, staring out. *What must they be thinking?* She quietly watched them. Then she turned to the difficult man across from her, asleep under the dusty Stetson. *What was he doing with Charlie and Candy?*

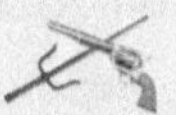

Stryker wasn't asleep. He had his own thinking to do. Had to work out some things, like those kids, Hearst, and whatever job he had, and Morgan. *Life had gotten damn complicated.*

Since the day Leigh was killed—died as he held her broken body. She'd said his name with her last breath. It had ridden on the blood flowing from her mouth. *Shit.* Yeah, since that day, life had been violent but simple, running from a murder he committed, and killing those who crossed him, *simple*. Like a wounded beast, snarling, dangerous, and deadly. At first, anger cut guilt, cut grief. Then anger faded, faded after he killed the man most responsible for Leigh's death. The other man who bore responsibility sat on the train, across from a woman and two kids, under a dirty black Stetson. *I should have double-checked the fucking coordinates.* Guilt and grief lingered unabated, no longer mitigated by anger. These days, no other emotions crossed his face. An efficient killer, he used deadly skills he'd acquired through the years, and stayed alive by instinct.

The God-damned nightmares. They haunted his sleep. The really bad ones hung around after he woke, especially those where he saw her lying on the ground, her clothing blackened by gunpowder. Bright red blood, Leigh's blood, on black powder. *Shit.* He'd given up on them ever ending.

Stryker used a forefinger and lifted the Stetson. The blue eyes of Miss Case were locked on him. Neither spoke. Just intensely stared. The children lay slumped together, exhausted, and fast asleep.

Finally, Stryker broke the silence. "You shot him."

"What you say? Shot who?"

"You're running. Not buying the door hinge shit. Now, tell me." Stryker's eyes narrowed to pale gray slits. "You kill your husband?"

Her lips tightened, and she shook her head. It wasn't convincing. The reddening of her face was.

"He was an asshole." Stryker deadpanned.

A curt dip of her head said *yes*. Stryker couldn't precisely tell what the clipped nod meant in addition to an affirmation of her husband's temperament. Miss Case let her head drop lower and kept it there. It seems as if–and it wouldn't be all that unusual–the woman could have been ashamed, either of her husband, or of herself for being married to an abusive man. Regardless, the woman being on the train meant she intended to put it behind her. He wouldn't complicate the effort. He let the matter drop.

"You have a place to stay." Stryker asked, as in another statement.

"I thought I'd find one when I got to San Francisco." Miss Case had caught on to the man's annoying habit of asking questions in a statement. Her eyes drifted to the scenery outside the window. Patches of the bay appeared between the conifers and cottonwoods. The clacking wheels counted the seconds until she said, "He wasn't an asshole when I married him." She spoke wistfully, as if sadly remembering a time when things were not so bad, maybe even good. Collecting herself, Miss Case sat upright, and returned to the present, to the coach and to the fearsome-looking man looking at her. "What kind of man are you?"

Stryker stared back at Miss Case and said nothing.

"All right, who is this other man we are to meet?"

"Name's Hearst, US Senator."

"Who *are* you?" Miss Case canted her head. "I need to know."

Stryker lowered the Stetson.

She searched the faces of Charlie and Candy, who were now awake and listening. They offered her shoulder shrugs. Miss Case settled back against the seat, staring at the man under the Stetson.

The rest of the journey to the city by the bay chiefly consisted of Miss Case learning about Charlie and Candy, asking them questions and receiving short answers.

Stryker kept the hat over his eyes, though. He stayed awake, listening. Miss Case did an admirable job of engaging the children when they became sullen, grieving over their dead parents.

As they approached San Francisco from the south, the flatlands by the bay seemed to have been scrunched together at the north end of the peninsula, creating the wrinkled hills on which the city sat. That is what happened, but the hills weren't caused by Pacific plate subduction under North America, rather they were caused by the Franciscan formation. Junk scraped off the Pacific plate during its subduction, that got transformed northward. Apparently, the stuff under the city is still pissed about being pushed around and has wrathful fits called earthquakes.

It was only a few months. However, in that short amount of time, San Francisco grew from a population of 1,000 in 1848 to 3,500 in 1850. Then, by1880, San Francisco had become a major city of 240,000 people. Like a giant living thing, it stretched out in all directions, particularly southward, gobbling up empty space. Not an evenly distributed spread, no rounded edge creeping outward, rather houses extended in curved strings, like the tentacles of a sea creature. Paris of the West, they called it. Political corruption, gambling, prostitution, and Shanghaiing were just growing pains. The era also gave birth to sewer lines, cable cars, and later the Golden Gate Bridge. Stryker had no reason to care one way or another, but he was surprised at the speed of growth.

Morgan placed the notice in the paper, and she would be waiting for him. She always had. He liked that. She must surely know. *Can't get too close. I've got to keep her alive. Damn jinx. Can't believe in that shit. Foolish stuff–ridiculous. Too rational for that. Still, I can't chance it. Won't ever chance it.*

The children were asleep. The book Miss Case read with them rested open on her lap. Charlie and Candy lay against her, puppies with an adopted mother. Her eyes closed, her head drooped, and she swayed gently with the rocking of the train. *Would she adopt the kids? Why do I care? The kids mean nothing to me. I should have left them in the coach.* Stryker looked out the window. He saw buildings come into view and then slide by. Closer together now, with small yards, which got even smaller as they rode over the hills and deeper into the city. And people, he'd only been in Pescadero for three-and-a-half months–*where the hell did they all come from? It's getting too crowded, damn it. Must be two hundred thousand here now!* (There were 298,997 in 1888.) The buildings were different too, more multi-level ones. He saw even larger structures out the other side of the train, built not with wood, but with stone and mortar, hulking shapes on hill tops, reaching higher to the sky. Many of the taller buildings were churches, erected so parishioners would have an attractive place to gather and worship and constructed magnificently for the glorification of what, Stryker didn't know. One has to admire, he thought, a man's ability to craft buildings spiraling to the city's clouds, but all in all, he preferred the tips of tall mountain pines tickling a clear blue sky. He sat back on the seat and wondered what kind of job Hearst had for him. The train slowed to a stop.

"Ferry House, San Francisco!" The conductor flung the door open and called from the doorway. He disappeared quickly. Jumped off the platform. Marched briskly up the line. No added information. Job over.

"Wait in front," Stryker instructed. Miss Case and the children rose and waited for their turn to file out of the coach. "Gonna tend my horse. Keep the kids with you. Won't be long."

Carol, who stood behind Charlie and Candy, and in front of Stryker, spun around to glare at him.

"Miss Case, I'm not taking off. Wait for me."

Her features softened. A smile twitched at the corners of her lips. Her blue eyes sparkled. "Carol. Stryker, please call me that."

Stryker nodded, dipping the Stetson.

The hulking Central Pacific engine rested, hissing steam bellows in front of the Ferry House. A wooden building, the Ferry House, was constructed in 1875 for trains coming into the city, and for ferries hauling passengers and freight, including locomotives, across the San Francisco Bay to and from Oakland. Carriages, buggies, horses, and a cable car waited for passengers arriving on the train.

People gathered there too, craning their necks to search for relatives, friends, or business contacts. They waved their arms when they saw them. Every man wore a business suit, and the women, they were outfitted in stylish bustled dresses, parasols, and all. Stryker had some-times wondered why women wore bustles. He'd been politely told bustles kept the backs of dresses from dragging on the ground. But the mixed breed had read about primates or monkey types in Africa with brightly colored asses. Presumably, nature made them that way to attract the opposite sex. Could it be, he speculated, a woman wore a bustle to make her ass look bigger for the same reason? Morgan never wore a bustle, and he liked that.

Of course, it was a cold, cloudy day, it's San Francisco. A light drizzle wet the cobblestones on the streets and made them glisten. Sunny summer days are a rarity in the City by the Bay. Fog had lifted though, and you could clearly see the bustling activity of a living San Francisco. "Places to go, people to meet, things to do." Stryker knew a captain in the Union Army who used to often say that before a cannon ball blew off his head. When Stryker stepped off the train in San Francisco, it always seemed as if he stepped into a different world. He could never feel comfortable in it, and he wondered now if Morgan and Hearst ever did.

Carol and the children stood alone at the depot. Thirty minutes passed before Stryker walked up. Why it took him thirty minutes to care for the roan wasn't mentioned, either by Carol or Stryker. Relief showed on the woman's face and the children greeted him with big smiles. And for the briefest of moments, Stryker thought, *so this is what it's like to come home to a family.*

Stryker, with his well-worn denims, ragged shirt, scuffed boots, dusty Stetson, and a .44 hung low on his hip, looked out of place in San Francisco. But the man would have looked more out of place in a three-piece suit. "Here comes another cable car," he said.

Charlie and Candy turned to watch it roll down Market Street, headed toward to the Ferry House. Stryker guessed it was the first time they'd seen one. If it excited them, they didn't show it. They'd seen a lot of new things lately. What's a cable car compared to the Central Pacific, gunfights, and the murder of their parents? So, Charlie and Candy merely watched the approaching tram without emotion.

Carol kept her eyes on Stryker. "Are we to meet the senator at the Palace now?" she asked.

"Yes." Stryker had had enough of kids. The sooner he got rid of 'em, the better.

"I won't discuss it now—in front of them, I mean," Carol said. "But I have a feeling what you're up to. Don't know how you will arrange it." She looked at Charlie and Candy, beamed a caring grin and said, "It'll be all right with me. They seem like good children."

Stryker hopped on the car first, stood on the step, turned, and extended a hand. Carol put her hands under Candy's armpits and lifted the girl to Stryker. Carol reached to help Charlie as well, but he hopped aboard without help. Stryker then extended his hand to Carol. The smile she flashed him and the warm crinkling by her blue eyes seemed lost on the mixed breed, not entirely, though. He grabbed her hand in a strong, yet gentle grip. The sensation surprised them both. They locked eyes.

It was one of those brief moments in time when surprise, possibility, rationality, disappointment, and then resignation flash through a person's mind. Scream to a peak and then fall off a cliff. It all showed, played out on Carol's face. His implacable countenance ended it.

"Thank you, Stryker." Warmth of the blue orbs turned chilly and the smile, now stale, faded away as well.

The street tram was near seating capacity. Cable cars had two separate seating arrangements, like those of a later age. The two main differences from more modern cars were, they had no enclosing outside walls and second, half of the benches were horizontal to the length of the car and half ran parallel facing outward along the sides. The newer cars had all parallel benches. The sections sat separated by a flimsy wooden wall, its upper half glassed with a door. The glass allowed the cable operator to see through the length of the car. Two three-foot handles rose from beneath the floor between a couple of parallel benches. The cable car was pulled along the street attached to an underground steel cable, and the operator clasped and released the cable by working the handles. A Scottish fellow named Hallidie got the cable car idea after watching horses being mistreated as they pulled wagons up and down San Francisco's hilly streets.

Carol squeezed Charlie and Candy in between two old sour-faced men seated on the front row of horizontal benches. The elderly gents grumbled a bit, but they shifted their butts and made room for the children. Carol sat in the middle of the second bench with two other women behind the children. Stryker scooted in next to frumpy middle-aged woman at the end of the third bench.

As the tram rolled up Market Street, the two women next to Carol got off at First Street and a dapperly dressed man got on. The handsome man appeared to be in his early forties and wore a gray pin-striped suit.

"Ma-am." He tipped his derby hat and sat beside Carol.

The cable car jolted forward.

"Haven't seen you on this run before." He canted his head toward her inquisitively with a big grin.

"No," she replied. "I'm new in San Francisco."

The fellow glanced at the next street coming up. "Where do you get off?"

"At the Palace Hotel." Carol's smile was slight.

"You're staying there?"

"No, I'm applying for work." She didn't know what else to say.

The eight stories of the Palace Hotel loomed three streets ahead.

"Say, if you're looking for work... can you sing? Oh, it doesn't matter. I own the Craven Café on the wharf, and I could use another girl on stage. He raised his eyebrows and looked approvingly down at Carol's legs. "Why don't you... hey, what the...!"

Stryker gripped his coat collar and dragged him across the bench. At the ornate safety railing, which was only five inches high, he pulled the man over the rail and threw him off the car. After rolling to a stop on the street's Kirill stones, the fellow rose to one elbow and watched the cable car lumber up the street.

"I shouldn't've gone back for the kids," Stryker mumbled.

Carol remained seated, facing forward. If she heard what Stryker said, she ignored it just like she ignored the café owner being thrown from the cable car. Strangely, none of the car's other occupants voiced an objection either. Either they knew the man who was thrown off and didn't like him, or they'd sized up Stryker and decided it was none of their business. Conversation on the tram was somewhat muted until the car stopped at the Palace Hotel and Carol, Stryker, and the two children stepped off. After the cable car continued up Market Street past Montgomery, riders spoke in hushed tones about what they'd just seen.

The Palace–that's what the locals called the eight-story, 755 roomed hotel. At the time, it was the most elegant hotel in the country, if not the world. Towering eight-story columns greeted guests who walked through the arched carriage entrance to the enormous grand court roundabout. At least a hundred large urns holding palms and giant ferns were stationed throughout the ground floor. In the cavernous lobby, polished marble and glazed granite covered the floors and walls. Rich mahogany woodwork complemented the stone, adding a touch of west coast elegance throughout the lobby, bars, and dining rooms. An elevator, then called a rising room, hauled guests up to their floors, a first on the West Coast. And another unique feature–each room had its own bath and toilet. First timers were simply overwhelmed with the wonderment of it all.

Carol, holding Charlie's and Candy's hands, entered the grand court behind Stryker. She stopped, staring awestruck at the grandeur. "My goodness!" She exclaimed. When she lowered her gaze to ground level, she saw Stryker walking under an archway to the expansive lobby. She hurried to catch up, dragging the children with her.

"Tell Hearst, Stryker's..."

"Yes, sir... here to see him," the desk clerk finished. The staff member, as well as the rest of the attachés, stood behind the imposing reception desk, a massive mahogany edifice, most of which towered over the tallest man. Only the middle of the forty-foot counter, where clerks checked in guests, was at waist level. Behind that was a large clock resting atop a ten-foot column, itself on a giant matrix of room drawers. The clerk reached under the counter and pushed a button buzzer to the largest luxury suite located on the eighth floor four times. Five seconds later, an answering buzz sounded.

"Go right up, sir." The clerk gave Stryker a courteous, albeit solemn, head dip.

Carol fell in behind the tall gunfighter who appeared so out of place in the magnificent hotel. Stryker embodied the opposite of extravagance. Socrates claimed one opposite generates the other. Stryker did his part.

More than a few hotel guests passing Stryker gave him quizzical looks; others gave him scorned glances and kept their distances. A couple of the women chanced nervous smiles. The Palace staff offered curt nods, knowing they would not be returned. Stryker ignored them all. However, an alert personage such as Miss Case would know Stryker was no stranger in the hotel. Indeed, the staff had seen the mysterious stranger several times in the hotel before, visiting privately or having dinner with Senator Hearst, and sometimes in the accompaniment of an attractive mining engineer. The hotel employees knew Stryker was to be accorded every courtesy and not asked questions. The mystery deepened when it was rumored whenever Stryker, or a man who looked a lot like Stryker, showed up in another town. There were always killings. However, the staff's questions about that remained in their throats.

The rising room.

They crossed the sprawling marble floor to a hallway and then stepped into a very small room. A uniformed attendant greeted them as they entered. The operator pulled the gate across the doorway and pushed a buzzer button on the wall. The gate was a matrix of metal strips, hinged on the ends so that it could be expanded and collapsed, and when expanded a person could see through it. Suddenly, the floor jolted beneath their feet, causing a slight buckling of the knees, and the floor outside fell. It might take a moment for a first-time rider to realize the outside floor wasn't falling. Their floor was rising!

Charlie and Candy tightened their grips and hugged closer to Carol. She, in turn, spaced her feet wider to steady herself. It was the first time for her too. The three of them watched in amazement as an outside room would drop from the ceiling and then disappear beneath them.

"Eighth floor," announced the attendant. The elevator slowed and came to a stop. The inside floor stopped level with the outside floor. The operator collapsed the gate.

Stryker led them out. "Come on."

Charlie broke away from Miss Case and ran out. He stomped on the carpet several times prior to turning and grinning at Carol and Candy.

They followed Stryker down the hall until they came to the senator's suite. On the way, Charlie stomped the carpet again. Stryker knocked on the door.

A young male attaché wearing a green blazer with gold colored "PH" initials on the pocket answered. He held an empty whiskey decanter tray by his side. "Mister Stryker." He swung the door wider for Stryker to enter.

Stryker passed by the attaché and saw the decanter and a sniffer glass on a drum table. The table had French artwork on its side latch door, and it sat between two maroon wingback chairs. Cognac was probably the chosen libation in the decanter. *"PH"* was etched on each glass. Miss Case gathered the kids close to her and marched in quickly behind Stryker. An open door on the far wall led to the bedroom. Both rooms softened footfalls with plush, forest-green carpeting. A mahogany conference table sat in the middle of the sitting room. Six dining chairs, two on the ends and four on the sides, provided seating for business meetings or group dining. On the left wall, a large, boxed window afforded a view of the city with the bay in the background. Two wingback chairs with the drum table between them faced the window, allowing comfortable seating for the views. A dark brown leather settee rested against the opposite wall. Two more wingback chairs, the same color as the other two, were clustered in the far corner with a small round table.

Hearst, who'd been standing by the window sipping cognac, turned to Stryker. A tall man, not as tall as Stryker, but he stood rail thin, and he wore a gray suit, sporting a full beard–gray as well, matching the suit. The nearly seventy years hung heavy on him, though his eyes were as bright and as intelligent as ever. Those eyes flashed a little wider when he saw Carol and the children. "Brought your family, Stryker?"

"Stage bandits murdered their folks," Stryker said. "The woman needs a place to care for them."

"I met them on the train," Carol added with a nervous smile.

Hearst shifted his gaze to Stryker.

You have a job for me, George."

"Ah, I see." The senator pursed his mouth firmly and nodded to Stryker as if he understood the implication. "All right, deal." He returned to Carol. "I'm sorry, Miss. Please sit. Would you care for a refreshment?" He looked at the kids. "And what are your names?"

"This is Charlie," Carol said, lifting the boy's hand, which she still held, toward Hearst. "And this is Candy." She signaled the same way with the girl's hand. She neglected to introduce herself.

A warm smile broke across the senator's rugged face. "I didn't get your name, Miss."

Carol blushed. "Carol Case."

"Please sit." Hearst gestured toward the settee. He watched as Carol and the children seated themselves. He reached under the conference table and pressed a buzzer. Immediately, the door opened, and the attaché entered. "Henry, bring us some milk and tea." Hearst motioned with his hand. "Wait, Henry. Send my buggy driver up." Henry spun on his heels and left, closing the door behind him.

"Do you have baggage?" Hearst asked Carol.

"I have only my carpetbag. The children have none," Carol answered.

"Are you married, Miss Case?" Hearst blurted out the question more awkwardly than he probably intended.

Carol glanced at Stryker and back to the senator. "I'm widowed."

"I'm sorry, Miss." The expression on Hearst's face showed he really wasn't.

Stryker stood near the conference table, thinking this thing may work out. He pulled out a chair and got comfortable.

A pause in the conversation ensued. Hearst stood smiling at Carol, and she tried not to squirm under his gaze.

Finally, the awkward moment was broken by Henry knocking on the door and entering carrying a tray. The buggy driver, an older man, perhaps in his fifties, followed Henry into the room. Smartly dressed, wearing a black tuxedo with tails and top hat; he clearly was not on the Palace staff.

"Matthew, wait for them to finish their tea and milk." Hearst, watching Henry fill the cups, said, "Take them to my house, Matthew. Tell Miss Fitzpatrick to make up two rooms at the end of the west hall. Miss Case and the children will stay there for the time being."

"Yes sir, Mister Hearst," Matthew replied sharply.

"And I think it would be a good idea for Charlie and Candy to have a few things, new clothes an' such. Inform Miss Fitzpatrick to see to it. Phoebe is in Europe with William. Won't be back 'til next year," Hearst said. He was talking to his driver, but he was looking at Miss Case.

Carol rose and placed her teacup on the tray. Henry, who'd remained standing stoically by the settee, gave Carol a polite nod. She glanced at Stryker, who dipped his head and bid her a two-finger salutation on the Stetson's brim. "Well then, we should be going." She took the empty cups from the children and sat them on the tray.

The children dutifully got to their feet. Tears welled up in Charlie's eyes, and he sniffled.

Carol noticed Charlie crying. She knelt in front of him and cupped his face in her hands. "What's the matter, Charlie?"

Tears welled up in the boy's eyes. He scrunched his face, trying hard not to bawl.

"It'll be all right, Charlie. We have to go with him. Your mother and father would want you to. They're watching over you now, I'm sure." Carol straightened and took hold of the children's hands.

Carol started for the door held open by Matthew, but Charlie stood firm, staring at Stryker.

Carol knelt by Charlie and followed the boy's gaze to Stryker. "Charlie? Is it Mister Man? What's... wrong?"

"Can he go with us?"

"No, I don't think so." She looked in Stryker's direction. Nothing there. She came back to Charlie. "Why Charlie?"

"He kills the monsters."

Groping for an adequate response to that one, Carol stammered, "Why, I'm sure if we need Stryker, he'll be there for us." She swung her head around, giving Stryker a quick frown, followed by arched eyebrows. "Won't you?"

"Yeah, yes I will, Charlie." *Ah, what the hell.*

"See," Carol said, standing and reaching once more for the children's hands. "Let's not hold everyone up." She led Charlie, who continued staring at Stryker, and Candy past Matthew into the hall. Henry left too, and Matthew closed the door after them, leaving Hearst and Stryker alone.

"You went noble," Hearst said, grinning.

"What's the job?"

CHAPTER FIVE

"Louis VIII cognac," Hearst said, as he poured cognac into the glass and gave it to Stryker.

Stryker took the cognac handed to him. "The job."

"Let's have a seat." Hearst motioned to the wingbacks. He'd heard how the fellow in the room with him slit throats. A shaky hand sloshed cognac onto the floor. He pretended not to notice. Even though he liked and respected Stryker, the man always made him nervous.

The senator sat and waited for Stryker to settle in the other wingback. "A long time ago, I was with a woman." He didn't mention if he was married then. "We got along well. She was awfully young. Pretty. I was forty-something. She might have been not quite twenty. I went off to work in the mines one spring. When I came back that fall, she was gone. Never saw her again." A hint of sadness crossed Hearst's face. He sipped from the glass and set it on the small table. "Now I hear a woman of the same name, Tami Tuit, is in Tahoe country." Hearst folded his hands together under his chin. He took a deep breath, looking pensive. "I think she's the same girl." A scowl came on the senator's face. "And I hear she's in trouble."

Stryker could tell that the woman, whoever she was, meant something to Hearst. But she'd be in her forties now. He wondered if the senator recalled a beautiful, lithe, young girl who may not be the same today. Happened before, he'd seen women put on two or three pounds a year, and their allure got swallowed in fat. "What kind of trouble?"

"She'd once told me she wanted to open a restaurant, a tavern, someday. The Tami in Tahoe opened a tavern. Tahoe Tami's, it was called. It burned down, I think she's been burned down two or three times. Fires weren't accidents. In fact, the second time they fired shots." He drew another long breath. "Heard she came to San Francisco for a while and then went back to Tahoe and opened a restaurant. Don't know how that went or if she's still alive. I got a letter, not signed. It might help you if you can find out who sent it." Hearst pulled out an envelope from inside his coat pocket. "Take it. Don't come back with it." Hearst handed the envelope to Stryker. "And another thing, Stryker, she must never know."

Stryker folded the envelope and stuck it in the back pocket of his denims. Stryker now realized why Hearst so easily agreed to take in Carol and the children. This job was no official charge or anything close to it. This was personal, a favor—a personal favor for an old man who still carried a torch for a woman. What the hell did he care about the senator's love life? No concern of his. In fact, he didn't care that much about the woman and the kids. He just wanted them out of his life. He looked at Hearst. He was sure Hearst tried hard not to show it, but his eyes were pleading. And *she must never know.*

"Headin' to Tahoe." Stryker set his glass on the little table and got to his feet.

Hearst remained where he was and watched as Stryker made ready to leave. Was he having regrets? Sending a man on what is probably a dangerous mission for his own remorse? He said nothing.

Stryker opened the door and there stood Morgan.

Rail thin with erect posture a drill sergeant would envy, Morgan wore her brunette hair parted on the side and down past her shoulders. High cheekbones accentuated the obsidian eyes and hollow cheeks. A hint of a smile rode on her lips. They were nowhere near full, *but they were damn kissable.* She carried her five-foot, seven-inch, one-hundred and fifteen pounds, with little effort. She wore a navy-blue jacket, open in front, and the white shirt underneath with an upturned collar was tucked into light-gray slacks. Underneath the shirt were a pair of firm breasts and a very flat stomach.

"Hello Stryker."

"Morgan." Stryker stepped into the hallway and shut the door behind him. He took Morgan's elbow and they started down the hallway.

"You leaving tonight?" she asked.

"Next train east."

"That won't be until the morning. I checked already." She patted the sun-tanned hand holding her arm. "Will you be gone long?"

"Don't know."

"Dangerous?"

"No." He knew she knew he was lying. From what Hearst told him, there would most likely be gunplay.

"Good."

Yeah, she knew all right. "Let's get something to eat."

They got to the rising room, but Stryker didn't ring for the lift, and he grabbed her hand when she reached for it.

Morgan turned to him with a puzzled look on her face.

Stryker brushed a strand of hair from her forehead and swept it behind her ear. "You're quite a woman, Morgan."

"Well... thanks, I... let's go eat outside the hotel," she stammered. No smile accompanied the suggestion.

No interruptions by Hearst. All right by me, Morgan. "Pick a place."

"Tadich Grill. California and Battery. We can take a cab if you don't wanna walk in your cowboy boots. It's four or five blocks."

The elevator gate opened. "Evening folks," the operator greeted.

When they stepped out of the rising room, Stryker took Morgan by the arm and guided her out the front onto Montgomery Street. There was a chill in the air and a slight breeze. Morgan buttoned her jacket. Drizzling rain chilled her hands, and she stuck them in her pockets. It hadn't occurred to Stryker to hold her hand, anyway. They walked up Montgomery past Sutter, Bush, and Pine to California Street, where they turned right. Old buildings, single story, had been torn down and new multi-level ones were built in their places. Real estate in San Francisco was becoming expensive. Another two and half blocks and they arrived at the Tadich Grill.

Inside the grill, dark mahogany wood dominated the room with masculine authority. Layers of cigar smoke hung heavy in the room. It was as if once a man entered the grill, he could only smoke cigars instead of cigarettes or pipes. The waiters served food spiced with salt, pepper, and cigar smoke. Even men who didn't normally smoke, and some women, would puff and twirl stogies. The Tadich Grill had tradition. The walls were covered with dark mahogany paneling on which kerosene lanterns sat perched on small platforms at eye level every three feet circling the grill. A rectangular bar with stools sat in the center where within the rectangle, bartenders slung drinks, whiskey mostly. Four wagon wheels hung from the ceiling; each wheel held six lanterns. Mahogany booths, head high, lined the left wall, and with two benches for seating, separated by a table inside each enclosure. A booth could accommodate six people. A few tables covered with linen and chairs sat between the bar and booths. No booths were on the right side, just stools by the bar. Pictures and ship ornaments hung along the wall. The kitchen, with the counter about chest high, was in the rear. An open walkway on the left side allowed servers access around the counter. The grill specialized in seafood, but it served steaks as well.

"Booth," Stryker said to the head waiter.

"Yes, sir. It's the last one. A big crowd is coming tonight. Follow me." The head waiter, a stout man wearing a white shirt with forest-green sleeve garters, spun smartly, and led them to the last booth in the back next to the kitchen. Upon seating Morgan and Stryker, and after offering menus printed on parchment paper clipped to flat boards, he asked, "Would you like something to drink first?"

"A Chardonnay if you have it," Morgan answered.

"Just got in a very good one from France, madam," the waiter said. "And you, sir."

"Coffee," Stryker grunted, not looking up from the menu.

While they waited, not much was said between the two. Neither was given to small talk. Finally, Stryker broke the silence. "How's the mining business?" The inquiry was unusual for him. He had an interest in her life, though. To what end his question would lead, he had no idea. He probed his own consciousness about how he felt about Morgan as much as he did her doings. Perhaps she might even mention something to engender a reaction from him. Maybe that's why he asked what seemed to be an innocuous question. Maybe it wasn't so benign.

"I'll be leaving soon for Mexico. George has land there, the Babicora Ranch in Chihuahua, and he wants me to explore its mining prospects. It will take some time. It's a 1,625,000-acre ranch. Why he bought it I haven't a clue. It is two hundred miles south of the border. I think it'll only be good for ranching and nothing else. One day, the Mexicans will simply confiscate it, anyway. (*Which they did*) I sail in three days," Morgan said, eyeing Stryker with a steady gaze.

"Who's going with you?" Stryker asked, expressing concern about her safety.

"George hired four armed guards. They will protect me and whatever gold I find. Curious why he didn't include you."

Stryker mulled that over before slinging out a reply. "The job I am heading out to do must be kept quiet. He couldn't send a detachment of men. Too public. Put off the gold trip." Implying he'd go with Morgan later.

"I could do that, but I won't. Here come the drinks."

"Here is your wine, ma-am." The very proper waiter, wearing a white jacket with a linen napkin draped on his forearm, set the tray on the table, and placed the glass of wine by Morgan. "And your coffee, sir." The coffee wasn't served with the same level of aplomb.

"Have you decided on your meal, ma-am?" The waiter picked up a pad and pencil from the tray.

"The halibut," Morgan said.

"Excellent, comes with scalloped potatoes and watercress. Will that be all right?"

Morgan nodded.

"And you, sir?" The waiter asked Stryker.

"Steak, medium rare, and potatoes–don't care how you cook 'em."

When the waiter left, the words wouldn't come, and awkwardness settled in. The grill room was crowded and noisy. The drinks flowed heavily, especially around the bar where every stool was occupied, and two or three men crowded around each stool, drinking and talking. Shouted orders to the kitchen and the clatter of returned plates added to the din. Regardless of the restaurant's clamor, the silence between Stryker and Morgan was deafening.

They took a few halfhearted bites of steak and fish and then laid their forks aside, appetites lost. Man and woman sat and gazed at each other, except for brief glances at passing waiters when the staring became too uncomfortable. There was no anger, or disagreement. It was just an awkward breach where words wouldn't come, not the right words anyway.

Finally, Morgan, still intensely eyeing him, said, "I could never love you simply for your virtue."

The word and what it meant had always been hiding in the tall weeds, waiting for one of them to pick it up. Taken aback by Morgan's declaration, Stryker tried to conjure up a weighty and worthy response. He couldn't. All he could do was sit there and stare at her finely shaped cheekbones.

Stryker was about to call for the check when the ruckus started. He tore his gaze from Morgan and leaned out from the booth to see who was doing all the shouting. He counted seven of them. Youths, at least they seemed young, teenagers maybe. They were small of stature, too small for full-grown men; and they wore black masks to hide their faces. Dressed in solid black tunics and matching black pajama-like trousers, he figured they were Asians. Two, maybe three, brandished pistols. Long knives or short swords were in the hands of at least three of them. Hard to tell. They were bunched together.

One of the black clad intruders, Stryker figured as the leader, yelled something in Chinese and pointed down the row of booths and the stools lining around the bar. The gang members broke out and darted to their assignments. They knew the drill. Each carried a weapon in one hand, a cloth laundry bag in the other, shouting, "Donate money!"

Confused by the gang member's requests—or orders—the first diners approached were slow to respond. Especially slow were the bar drinkers.

They'd soaked up a drink or twelve and seemed unsure whether this was a robbery or a prank to raise money for some unknown cause.

A fat man on a bar stool with a handle-bar mustache was among the first customers accosted by the intruders. Stryker couldn't see the booth diners to see how they fared. He watched the fat man. The fat man probably had closer to the twelve beers rather than the two. He'd spun around on the stool to face the Asian youth yelling at him. When demanded he "donate" money, he slurred something unintelligible and dropped a single coin in the laundry bag. More yelling. It looked as if the fat man's lips mouthed "Fuck you..." and some words Stryker couldn't make out, and then "bastard."

That's when the gang leader stepped up and shot him in the chest. Even the thieves jumped at the sudden roar of the gun.

The fat man spun back around and took one last drink of beer. Then he slumped against the counter and died.

The Asian who'd first demanded money moved on to the next bar customer. Bag out, gun pointed, "Donate weal money!" The Asian thief had trouble with his "R"s. Regardless, the next fellow understood and was more generous. He dropped a wad of US currency in the laundry bag.

Stryker suspected none of the customers except him was armed. The thieves probably counted easy prey in the restaurant. He settled back into the booth and pulled the Peacemaker. He cocked the hammer and waited.

Morgan scooted to the wall and hunkered down, trying to make herself small.

A few minutes passed, and Stryker heard the Asian solicitor come to the booth next to them. "Donate money!" He yelled to diners in the booth.

While holding the laundry bag open to receive "donations," the robber peaked around the wall. Only his head showed and the .44 slug blew out a large chunk of his brains. The blast knocked the thief backward, and he fell between two bar drinkers hunched over their drinks, hoping not to be noticed. The dead thief's rude intrusion caused them to spill their drinks and they cursed the loss.

The grill room suddenly became silent.

Stryker, in the meantime, re-cocked the Peacemaker and rose from the table. But before he could get out of the booth, a shotgun boomed. Then there was a second blast.

A quick glance to his left and Stryker saw a man; maybe the owner/manager, stout body, looked to be in his fifties, burr cut hair, maybe an old drill sergeant, coming out of the kitchen holding a breeched shotgun. He calmly pulled the two spent shells, letting them drop to the floor, and smoothly angled-seated two new shells in the chamber. Stryker turned his attention forward. Three black-clads lay on the floor, blood spreading from under the bodies. Two weren't moving. One crawled toward the door, leaving a crimson trail behind his black cotton shoes. Stryker held back, remaining by the booth and out of the shotgun's line of fire. He fired two more well-placed shots from where he stood, putting lead in another two robbers. The shotgun roared again.

Seven down. One still moving. Stryker turned to the shotgun holder and held up a palm. He made long strides to the front of the bar, stepping over bodies, and fired a round into the head of the crawler.

He returned to the booth with Morgan. "That's all of 'em," he said, dropping down on the bench across from her.

"Your meal is on me," the shotgun toter said, appearing at their table.

"You ex-military?" Stryker asked.

"Yes."

"Shows." Stryker turned to Morgan who was still hunched down. "Let's go, Morgan."

The drizzling rain stopped, but distant thunder rumbling from the north warned of a brewing storm. A chilly breeze swirled a little stronger than before. They stepped in pools of light cast by illuminated shop windows and their shadows would leap up beside them and disappear when they left the light. Morgan turned up her collar and plowed her hands into her pockets again. She had an erect posture, purposeful stride. *Damn, she was attractive.* The wind blew from the front and swept the hair from her face. Stryker couldn't help but stare—a slightly curved forehead, an elegant neck, those sculpted cheekbones, and lips that felt like butterfly wings when she brushed his chest with her kisses.

"Stryker, you shot those men—those boys—so... like some kind of an inhuman machine. No flinching, no… and so cold." Morgan stopped walking and faced him. "I shouldn't complain, and I'm not. But you scare me sometimes."

Stryker stopped too.

When he made no reply, she resumed walking. "Stay with me tonight, Stryker. Stay with me and hold me."

They walked the rest of the blocks to the Palace without speaking. About halfway there, Morgan withdrew a hand from her pocket and slipped it into his. Stryker felt embarrassed. He never enjoyed holding hands. He didn't pull away, though. He gripped her hand tightly and only let go to open the hotel door, but then he never returned it. Out of the corner of his eye, he saw Morgan smile to herself.

Inside the Palace Hotel, several events were happening, a wedding, a retirement celebration, and a birthday party for a banker's daughter. The place was crowded with happy, boisterous celebratory guests dressed in formal tuxedos and beautiful gowns, and they were sloshing lots of spiked punch down their throats. Morgan would have probably been asked to join any number of joyful groups clustered in the Grand Hall, but not the man beside her. His fierce countenance intimidated, and warned that joy was not in him, never had been, never would be. Morgan and Stryker headed for the redwood-paneled rising room.

"Third floor, please," Morgan said.

The elevator attendant was about to slide the expandable door closed when a man yelled, "Hold on, sir!" Running, and trying not to spill a champagne glass of punch, the young man pulled a girl stumbling on high heels behind him. The splotch of pink-red stain on his white ruffled shirt may have explained why the glass was half full. They poured into the lift, panting and laughing. "Third floor, please." The fellow puffed. He saluted Stryker with the glass and tried to gather himself. The girl, who appeared to be in her early twenties, averted her eyes and stared at the floor.

Stryker stared impassively at them, Morgan offered a faint smile, and the elevator attendant watched the floors go by.

"I'm Boz, I go by Boz anyway," the young man said with a wide grin. "And this is my wife, Mitzy. We were in the wedding party down-stairs. I was best man. Mitzy was Maid of Honor."

Stryker figured Boz mentioned "wife" for Mitzy's benefit. Stryker had already noticed her ring, though. She was a pretty thing, shy smile and all. Boz, had an air of easy confidence and one could tell he was an ambitious fellow on his way up.

"Third floor," the operator announced. He opened the gate.

The young couple allowed Morgan and Stryker to step into the hallway first. Stryker wondered if that made Morgan feel old. He glanced behind him and saw Boz putting the key in the second door on the left from the lift, room *303*.

Morgan noticed his backward glance and said, "We're at the end, *340*."

Hearst, had as usual, arranged for Stryker's lodging at the Palace, however Stryker hadn't inquired at the front desk about it. At this point, he figured he wouldn't need the room. Morgan handed him the key, and he opened the door.

A lantern sat on the desk, already lit, and turned down low. Stryker turned it up and lit another lantern.

"Care to freshen up, Stryker?" Morgan's question suggested he needed to. "Towels in the bathroom." The Palace Hotel was one of the first hotels anywhere, with individual bathrooms in each room. "I'll read the paper while you do." Morgan leisurely lifted the *San Francisco Examiner* off the desk. She sat in the only cushioned chair in the room and began reading the headlines.

Stryker took his time in the bath. He shaved and after filling the tub with hot soapy water, he lowered his body into the suds and soaked his muscles for several minutes prior to lathering up. He'd seen Morgan pick up the *Examiner* and rightly concluded she wouldn't be joining him in the tub. She had at other times, not tonight though. Twenty minutes later, he emerged from the bathroom wearing a man's terrycloth bathrobe with a large "*P*" on the pocket.

"I'll just be a minute," Morgan said, as she passed him on the way to the bathroom. She closed the door. Stryker figured she would then go about doing those mysterious preparations women do in the bathroom.

They seemed to always take longer than they should, but he'd never ginned up enough impudence to ask a woman what the hell she did in there. He heard running water and glass bottles set on the sink. Odd, he thought, a man never heard the bottles get lifted. He only heard glass things clink on the sink–which added to the mystery. He stretched out on the bed.

Morgan finally emerged from the bathroom. She wore a woman's terrycloth robe (a much smaller one), with a "*P*" on the pocket. She saw Stryker lying on the bed. She tilted her head and gave him one of those heartfelt, affectionate smiles of understanding only a woman can give. She blew out the lanterns and climbed on bed beside him. The slight shaking of the bed woke him up.

"Let's get under the covers," she whispered.

They rolled to the sides of the bed, stood, and shed the robes. Stryker slipped back into bed between the cool sheets and under the fluffy bedcover. He lay on his back and curled an arm around Morgan, who nestled in beside him. She rested her head on his shoulder and lightly caressed his chest.

His hand encircled the back of her neck, gently massaging both sides. After a few minutes, his fingers traced down the nape of her slender neck and out to a bony shoulder. The tips of his fingers followed along the bones and down to a shoulder blade. Bones... Morgan was not skinny, but she was thin, and in good shape. He liked the way she felt, delicate bones under a velvet layer of skin. Certainly not fleshy like a lot of women he'd felt... *and fucked*. He didn't feel like *fucking* Morgan tonight. He just wanted to lie there in bed and caress her very fine bones. *Jesus, what the hell was wrong with me? I just want to feel her bones? I must be one crazy bastard.* Stryker drew his hand back up to the nape of her neck, just beneath the hairline, and resumed a light massage. *Well hell, if every man had the same likes, somewhere in the world I reckon there'd be a tired, worn-out woman.*

A few moments later, Morgan's breathing had the regular exhalation of a person asleep. Her hand rested motionless on his chest. He lay there thinking, in the morning he'd leave her. It'd be a long time before he held her like this again. A sudden shudder went through him–*maybe never.* It took over two hours before Stryker finally drifted off to a trou-bled sleep.

Morgan mumbled something when he rolled away from her and got out of bed. He didn't want to wake her, so he chose not to ask her to repeat it. It was better that way. Goodbyes were damned awkward. He got dressed in the bathroom and slipped from the room. Light from the hallway allowed him to take one last look at the small shape curled up in the bed when he left.

A commotion in the hall, muffled voices, footfalls, had intruded into another agonizing nightmare about Leigh, and woke him out of the dream. He carried no watch, but an internal clock told him it was time to get up, get ready, and leave for the train. Out in the hall, a small crowd of people, two in police uniforms, and the rest dressed as hotel staff, were gathered by the door of the young couple's room. A woman in a maid's uniform, who stood closest to the doorway, cupped a hand over her mouth. Her hand and a furrowed brow suggested whatever she saw inside was unpleasant. As Stryker passed the room on his way to the elevator, one of the police officers shooed the onlookers away from the doorway. Stryker glanced inside and stopped walking.

An elderly man and a woman sat slumped in two chairs very close together and in the middle of the floor. They'd been shot in the head. Stryker checked the room number on the door–*303*. It was the same room the young couple had entered the night before. The old woman's head slanted away from the man next to her. It looked as if she'd been shot in the temple. The man's head tilted backward. There was lots of blood, but the revolver in his lap looked as if it had been held and fired from under the man's chin. Stryker continued walking and got on the elevator. Stryker was positive it was the young couple's room and although it made little sense, he couldn't help wondering if a red wine stain lay under the blood on the old man's shirt.

"Say, what do you think went on in there?" the uniformed operator asked, as he lowered the car to the first floor. "I heard about the deaths."

"Time flies when you're happily married," Stryker said, getting off the elevator.

"Huh?" the operator stammered, staring at Stryker walking away

Morning crept into the day as a dark, cloudy sky. A light rain fell from the heavens, making streets glisten. Men worked outdoors on the streets, getting horses and carriages outfitted. Shopkeepers set their wares under awnings in front of the stores. They went about their tasks in stoic silence. Living in San Francisco, they'd learned to tolerate the wet dreary days, but they weren't cheerful about it. There were times when the city by the bay felt like the city *in* the bay. This was the day which greeted Stryker when he walked out of the Palace Hotel that morning. It fit.

He took the cable car to the train depot. A cold north wind swept the rain inside the open tram. Early morning riders on bench seats hunched their shoulders and turned away from the rain. Men wearing hats, dipped them toward the weather to keep water from running down their necks, and females, mostly working-class girls, clutched newspapers over their heads. Their class wore no hats. Stryker stood at the rear of the car, preferring to have the rain soak his legs and boots rather than his upper body. The roof of the cable car blocked the rain if you stood in the back and were tall enough. Stryker, on his own, could concentrate on what lay ahead. He glared through the cable car and into the rain, and beyond the rain. He thought about his travel plans and how he would deal with the senator's woman when he got to Tahoe.

The woman he'd left in a warm bed had just awakened to find him gone.

The Central Pacific ticket agent at the Fourth and Brannan Streets depot saw Stryker step from the cable car and sent a runner after the roan. He'd come to know that much about the tall stranger. Stryker's fearsome countenance did not invite questions, but several times in the past year, the agent had seen him arrive by ferry or train, stable his horse, and get on a cable car. A day or two later he'd come back, gather the roan, and leave town.

"Where to, sir?" The agent asked. The man in the ticket window wore a dark blue uniform and a matching blue Bell Crown cap with "C. PAC." stitched above the short bill. The name tag on his chest pocket said, "Jeff."

"Truckee."

"Three dollars and twenty cents if you're taking the train all the way. I sent for your horse. Be another dollar for the animal."

Stryker dug out four one-dollar notes, two Seated Liberty dimes and handed them through the window. "The seven thirty-five on time." Stryker asked the question in a statement.

"Yes, sir." Agent Jeff shoved a faded print ticket with "**Central Pacific-July18-Truckee**" and **22467** stamped on it through the window. "And this is for the horse." He slapped one-half of a perforated tag on the counter and shoved it to Stryker.

Stryker put both in his shirt pocket and went inside the depot to wait on his horse. After buying a mug of hot black coffee in the café, he waited by a window. Fifteen minutes later, he saw a stable boy bringing up the roan, saddled and ready. He looked around at the people waiting to board the train. There were men in suits and derby hats, women with outsized dresses with bustles and big fancy hair–wigs. Stryker figured they had to be New York, Boston, or Chicago travelers, showing how much better they were than westerners. They acted and spoke like it too, haughty, with snarky comments to those not in their party. Stryker speculated if the women showing off their bustles secretly liked it up the ass– why else would they try to make their butts look bigger? And he also questioned if the men cried easily. He threw the last of the coffee down his throat and went to the horse car to watch the roan get loaded.

Satisfied with the roan and what was on it, saddle, bedroll, Winchester .44, Stryker walked out of the car and down the ramp to wait on the platform. The rain had let up, but a thick fog rolled in to smother the streets and enshroud the buildings, including the train depot, in its heavy wet mist. Even the train disappeared now. He could only see one coach car at a time. The big SP Twelve-Wheeler sat rumbling on the tracks, and its reverberations ran through the boards beneath his feet.

Stryker had made the trip over the Sierras several times in the past year for Hearst. Once in snow so deep the train couldn't punch through and they had to use bucker plows to clear the tracks. The trip, including stops along the way, took the better part of twenty-four hours on a good day, sometimes forty-eight or more on snow days.

Rather than wait in the depot, he boarded early. As he walked from the platform and toward the front of the train (Stryker always preferred a coach car near the engine) he passed a car unlike the rest of the rest of coaches–an-add on. He couldn't read all the lettering on its colorful side, but he could make out **"Circus"** written in big red letters. In fact, there were two of those cars. He went farther up the line until he saw the rear of the hulking locomotive and climbed in the lead coach. The car was empty. As usual, Stryker selected a seat in the last row, his back against the rear wall. The coach was one of the newer train coaches being outfitted these days, with instead of hardwood bench seats; this car had individual leather cushioned seats. He settled in the last row aisle seat, depot side. Stretching out his long legs ahead of him, he lowered the brim on the Stetson.

After years in the Army, the Civil War, the Indian Campaigns, and nights under the stars, part of Stryker's brain rested while in a remote outpost of his mind, a sentry stood guard, wired to his senses. The sentry monitored the Twelve-Wheeler's regular steam blasts, while remaining alert for new sounds. They came. First, the conductor's shout to board from the belly of the fog, then shortly afterward, he heard people's voices begin as a low murmur, then grow louder and more discernible as they boarded the train.

Stryker heard a beautiful, mellifluous voice. Usually, he didn't use ten-dollar words, even in his head. This time, he made an exception. Light and sweet, it was, and with an accent he couldn't quite make.

"Save a seat for me, Krull," she sang out to a man so named who had the good judgment not to reply. "I'm taking a moment to see the cats," she added. A man's voice in reply, or anyone's for that matter, would be like following Beethoven's *Moonlight Sonata* with a fart–or in Stryker's case, a bullet. (That does not infer the mixed breed didn't like good music.)

The coach filled seats front to rear and the only available seats when Krull, a scruffy-looking man who looked to be in his fifties, made his way down the aisle, were by Stryker. When the fellow got to the last row, he stopped and looked back up at the coach, searching for another empty seat. Seeing none, he shrugged his shoulders and stepped over Stryker's legs to sit by the window. He glanced at the man with the long legs across from him, noting the .44 on his hip, and then stared out the window, looking for his female companion in the fog.

Krull was a short man. He had unkempt, gray matted hair with grody yellow strands throughout the straggly clumps. He pasted his face to the glass and watched out the window for the girl. Upon spotting her, he banged on the glass with a fist blackened with coal dust. To be truthful, it wasn't coal dust. Krull seldom bathed.

The girl heard the rapping and waved. A short time later, she appeared at the far end of the coach and, holding a cloth carry bag in front of her body, came down the aisle and sat beside Krull, facing Stryker. His crossed legs stretched out between the girl and Krull. Had Stryker lifted the Stetson, he would have seen an attractive girl, slim in stature, maybe nineteen years old, angular face, wearing square horn-rimmed glasses. She had on olive wool slacks, a gray cardigan sweater, and a forest-green thigh-length Victorian jacket. Her hair pulled back in a bun, she looked studious. She sat and studied the long-legged man across from her.

The train couplings clanked together prior to one last passenger boarding the train. Stryker, watching out the window, saw a young man burst into the coach, breathing heavily, as if he'd just completed a sprint race. Indeed, he had. He'd raced on foot alongside the train until he could leap onto the coach steps.

"Whew! Made it!" He exclaimed, laughing. Surveying the car, he saw only one open seat, the one by a man snoozing in the back. He started for it. As he walked past each row, sometimes having to grip a seat back to maintain his balance in the lurching car, he offered sheepish grins to the staring eyes. He reached the last row. "Excuse me, sir."

Stryker tipped his weathered Stetson back with a forefinger.

"Is this seat taken?"

"Sit down."

The young man sat. Turning to Stryker, he extended a hand and said, "Name's James. Glad to make your… uh, acquaintance.

Stryker lowered his hat in the middle of the salutation.

"Well, I guess…" James looked across the narrow aisle; saw the girl staring at him. "Good morning, Miss. I'm James, and you're?"

"Katina," she replied with a guarded smile. She directed an open hand to her companion, "My friend and mentor, Krull."

'I'm going to Philadelphia to complete my studies," James said with a broad smile.

"That's nice," said Katina. "You have a profession in mind?"

"Business, finance–at the Wharton School of Business, University of Pennsylvania; it's the first of its kind in the world," James boasted. He sat up straighter, looking very proud. Upon seeing the pair across from him as unimpressed, he asked, "And where might you be headed?"

"Truckee," Katina answered.

"Truckee?" James questioned, as if to imply a Truckee destination meant a failing of some measure.

"Yes, Truckee," Katina huffed. "My father was a ring-master for Ringling Brothers–and a lion tamer, a very famous lion tamer, he was. Maybe not here in America." Katina cleared her throat. "In Europe, you see, he was known all over Europe." She glanced at Krull and then turned back to James.

"You said he was. Is your father deceased now?"

"Two years ago."

"Sorry. An illness or… I hope it was peaceful, I mean."

"He was killed by one of the cats."

"A cat?"

"Yes, a lion. In fact, one of the lions is in the car behind us. He left me the cats, all three of them." Katina paused. She stared at James, who appeared lost for words. "Look, mister–whatever your last name is, I don't have much money. My father left me nothing but the lions. That's really all he had. I travel around and charge for people to see 'em. Pay me a dime and you can go look."

"Well, I'll be going on… uh, pardon me… Katina, I take your mother is… too?"

"Died of cholera when I was four."

"Penney, James Penney's my name."

"Bourgeoisie class," Katina huffed. She turned to Krull. "You can always tell."

"Excuse me?" James asked. His facial expression was pleasant enough.

"Wealthy capitalist." The girl grew haughty.

"I'm not wealthy yet. I sure hope to be, though," James beamed.

"Yes, get rich on the backs of the oppressed, the working class. Greedy capitalist."

Krull remained silent, watching and listening to his protégé. It was not hard to see, he was pleased.

"Well, I don't know about…" James began.

"All capitalists are greedy. That's why capitalism must be vanquished. Communism is the only way to do it and free the masses," Katina snapped.

"Aren't they free now?"

"Of course not! They're enslaved to the rich. Their minds and bodies, their lives, are bent in servitude to the upper class. The impoverished working class, the proletariat, toil their lives away for the rich. And the rich–they only give the poor pennies and religion. Religion to believe they'll have a better afterlife if they toil in abject misery in this world. So, the rich give them God and ornate churches."

"I don't see it that way." James sounded offended.

"I'm sure you don't."

"You don't, you don't believe in God?"

"No, you fool. God, religion, is opium for the masses. To be truly free, the oppressed must share equally in what's produced, the wealth accumulations–and weaned from religion, from God." Katina sat back in her seat, letting that sink in James.

"I don't think people will vote for that," James ventured. He sounded unsure of himself.

"To move the world from feudalism to capitalism to socialism to communism will require violence. But the wondrous, classless utopia will be worth it." The girl smiled kindly.

"Atheistic Communism? A lot of people might die fighting against that."

"Millions will die," Krull spoke up. "The world must rid itself of everything, everybody, who stands in the way of achieving true Communism. Think of it as a cleansing," Krull stated with authority, and as a matter of fact.

"But I want to achieve. I want to be the best I can. Not just to make money, I want my efforts to be rewarded. I would need to feel like I've done something with my life. You make it sound like everyone would have to be the same." James abandoned talk of death and religion and took it to his personal philosophy. There was no hesitancy in him now.

"You'd have to get over that," Krull said. "Otherwise, you'll be swept out in the cleansing."

"You have family, Krull?" James tried to change the discussion.

"My wife and seven children are in London." Krull shifted uncomfortably.

"You see them often? I mean, do you miss them?" James asked.

"My work is important."

"What kind of work do you do?"

"I write and study. I've been widely published."

"Would I know of…?"

"A *Communist Utopia*. You must read and study it."

"You make a lot of money with it?" James asked enthusiastically.

"I support us while he writes and teaches." Katina interjected haughtily.

James reclined against the seat cushion. He glanced beside him at the dozing mixed breed and decided to work on a nap as well.

Stryker, who'd been listening to it all under the Stetson, thought about the two people across from him, and decided to kill them both.

Hours passed and conversation never picked up again. When they stopped in San Jose, Katina got to her feet and went out, presumably to check on the lions. Krull remained seated, scribbling furiously in a book.

Stryker, who'd raised his hat while Katina tended the cats, eyed the girl a few minutes later as she came down the aisle. As he watched, he wondered if he would hate her without having heard what she told James. There's something about a person that can piss a man off just by looking at him or her. Kind of like animal instinct, he thought, and the girl pissed him off.

She plopped down and said to Krull, "That's the last of the pigs."

Krull said nothing, didn't look up to comment, and kept writing.

Stryker figured the pigs were cat food. Outside, he heard the train's couplings clang in sequence down the track. The coach jolted forward, and as he looked out the window, the town of San Jose slid by.

A little later, Katina looked up and saw Stryker glaring at her. She froze, appearing petrified. You could tell. Fear was pasted on her face, awestruck by his fierce countenance. If she indeed felt fear, she had good reason. She withdrew a book and stuck her nose in it. Krull remained busy with his scribbling.

Things stayed that way until well into late afternoon. Krull and Katina were busy with their literary pursuits. James slumped away from Stryker, quietly snoozing, And Stryker–his mind was busy thinking of ways to thwart the societal utopia envisioned by the scraggly man across from him. Death would figure in it. After considering several possibilities, Stryker picked up the San Francisco *Examiner* and opened it to read the headlines. Bored, he read the paper from front to back.

They were headed northwest now, snaking along the tracks east of the San Francisco Bay toward Stockton. Running twenty miles an hour, it took the iron horse roughly four hours to go from San Jose to Stockton. Most of the other passengers had exhausted conversations and had immersed themselves in reading something or were napping. They were about an hour out of Stockton when Katina broke the silence and asked Stryker a question. Katina had caught Stryker looking at her.

"Are you interested in politics?"

"Not your shit."

That ended the talking. Katina and Krull didn't even speak to each other for the rest of the trip. Evidently, the two of them correctly surmised Stryker could become violent.

When the Central Pacific pulled into Stockton, Katina rose and got off the coach. Stryker saw her walk past and figured she was going to tend the lions again. Several other passengers got off as well. New passengers boarded, about half as many as those who'd disembarked. Some ventured toward the rear of the coach and a few empty seats remained, peppered throughout the coach. James offered an embarrassing smile to Stryker as he rose to take up residence in a seat closer to the front.

A short time later, the *"all aboard"* call was made, and the train began a slow rollout of Stockton. No Katina. Krull scooted over to the window and pressed his cheek on the glass to search for the girl. He shot a nervous glance at Stryker, jumped to his feet, and scurried to the back door. A few moments later, Krull returned and slumped down in his seat. Stryker figured the lazy bastard had never got off the coach. He probably stood on the rear platform to look for the girl. Visibly agitated, Krull picked up his writing tablet and then cast it aside. He moved over by the window and stared through the glass. He sat like that for the next fifty miles to Sacramento. They stopped briefly in Lodi. Mail bags were quickly exchanged and the train started up again before Krull could exit the car.

Finally, upon the train halting in Sacramento, here the big engine rested longer, belching loud puffs of steam. The population in Sacramento had grown to 26,000. The town sat on the confluence of the American and Sacramento Rivers and had continued to flourish after the gold rush. Named after the Spanish word for sacrament, Sacramento became the state capitol in 1879. The railroad, more so than the rivers, sponsored the town's growth and modernization. It even had electric lights these days and was a bustling stop for train travelers.

Krull rose and got off the coach. Stryker followed. The lions were in a run-down circus car three back from theirs. Its faded lettering and show mural were barely recognizable on the sides of the converted boxcar. There was no longer a traveling circus inside, just the old three lions—three hungry old lions. Krull and Stryker climbed the coach steps at the front end, opened the door, and entered.

Inside the car, the only light came from the doorway and narrow ventilation slats. Even through the murkiness, they were able to see the horrifying scene by the lion's cage. Katina, or what was left of her, lay by the cage. She had either stuck an arm through the bars or one of the lions snagged it because the arm was gone. The rest of her body lay outside the bars, but her face and neck had been eaten. Only part of her skull with remnants of matted hair remained. One couldn't tell if the head was still actually attached to body. Katina's back was a bloody mess. The lions had evidently reached through the bars and clawed away her clothing to strip off the flesh from her backbone and ribs.

The three lions lay at the far end of the cage, warily eyeing the two men who'd just entered the car.

Stryker grabbed Krull by his collar and dragged him to the cage door. The latch was a sliding mechanism with an iron ring, and a slotted plate hinged over it. There was no lock. Stryker opened the latch, shoved Krull in the cage, and shut the door. Strangely, Krull didn't yell. He grumbled something about not wanting to be in the cage with "these beasts." The lions hadn't yet moved from where they lay, but now their eyes were locked on the intruder.

Stryker grabbed Katina by an ankle, and re-opened the cage door. He gripped the body by the belt on the wool slacks and heaved it into the cage.

Krull turned around and gruffly demanded, "Let me out of here!" He leaped over Katina's body and stuck his arm between the bars, fumbling furiously with the latch. All three cats attacked at once. They knocked Krull to the floor and whatever he screamed was drowned out by angry growling of the lions tearing into him.

Stryker eyed the dinner scene impassively. "Make sure they get an equal share, Krull," he said, as he left the car.

The Central Pacific pulled out of Sacramento, and Stryker sat alone, snoozing in the back of the coach. A half hour passed and he surmised the big cats had finished dinner. The circus car was private, and it shouldn't be inspected for at least another day or two. Bones and clothing would probably be all that was left of Krull and Katina. It wasn't until the stop in Colfax when Krull and Katina failed to re-board the coach that James came back to sit across from Stryker.

He waited twenty minutes before getting up the nerve to interrupt Stryker's nap. "Sir?"

Stryker tipped the Stetson from the bridge of his nose and sat up.

"The girl and the old man." James shifted his butt in the seat. "They got off the train? I don't see 'em. I mean, I haven't seen either since Sacramento, and I was just kinda wondering…"

"They're feeding the lions."

"Oh, I guess they decided to stay with them for a while."

"Reckon so." Stryker allowed.

'I think that old man got that girl brainwashed, don't you?"

"James, go on to college. Get your degree like you said. Get a job. Work hard. Achieve your potential. Make a good living. Marry a woman who thinks like you and raise a family. Forget that girl. She's not for you." Strange and unusually verbose advice offered by the mixed breed.

"You don't think she's for…"

"The lions ate 'em."

James's mouth gaped open. His eyes widened in dismay. He scooted forward, nearer to Stryker, and lowered his voice. "The lions... they ate them?"

Stryker nodded.

"My God." Then James whispered. "Did you see it?"

"The girl was dead when I got there, and then Krull went into the cage with the lions."

"Why'd he do that? Because of her death, you think? He kill himself?"

"I threw him in."

Stryker settled back in the cushioned seat, lowered the Stetson, and stretched out his legs.

James scooted rearward against the backrest and studied the man across from him for several minutes before laughing out loud.

CHAPTER SIX

Conversation between James and Stryker stayed light and sparse up and over the Sierras. James moved by the window and busied himself looking at the spectacular landscape. On occasion, he tried to strike up more of a conversation with the taciturn Stryker, perhaps emboldened by the wordy advice given earlier.

"I was out here visiting for the summer. How about you, mister?" James ventured at one point.

"Going to Truckee."

"Home?"

"No."

"I traveled to San Francisco by ship. First time seeing all this. These mountains are sure something, aren't they?" James smiled broadly, admiring the view. He received no comment from the mixed breed. "Are the Rockies as big?" Again, he got nothing. "Perhaps I'll spend a few days in Colorado. I'd like to see more of them if they are, than just seeing 'em from the train." James was talking to himself now. He'd given up on Stryker.

They passed over the Sierras, making a brief stop at the roundhouse and the Cardwell Hotel. After passing through Summit tunnel, the longest tunnel in the Sierras at 1750 feet, they continued down the east side of the range.

"Nice to meet you, sir," James said.

Stryker rose, dipped the Stetson, and stepped off the train. Outside, the sign hanging above the station door read, *"Welcome to Truckee, elevation 5,817 feet."*

Stryker strode by the window where James sat watching him. The killer went on to the livestock car, brought the roan down the ramp, and climbed in the saddle. He never saw James Cash Penney again.

James went on to Colorado and stayed for a while. He got a stockroom job in a small western chain of department stores, making $25 a month. J.C. Penney never attended college. He eventually did well enough to buy his own store. Later, he expanded, creating an empire of over 1,400 stores nationwide, and at one point, he taught another young man who was interested in the retail business how to wrap packages. That young man's name was Sam Walton.

Truckee was still very much a lumber town. Long lines of freshly-cut logs that were floated down the river from the Tahoe basin, had been pulled out and stacked by the train tracks, waiting to be loaded on flat cars headed over "the hill" to San Francisco. Some smaller ones were used to build fires for men to stand around and drink at night. Not many women lived or even traveled through Truckee. Most of the few women who called Truckee home, occupied houses on Jibboom Street where they plied their prostitution trade. But times were changing now, and Truckee was slowly evolving into a tourist stop on the way to Lake Tahoe. Hotels were no longer just for the lumber men to sleep, where beds were occupied by different men continuously throughout the night. Some rooms were now reserved for the gentile class, especially women.

Stryker certainly wasn't in the gentile class, but he preferred a clean bed. He stabled the roan and paid for its groom and feed. He pulled the carbine from its boot, threw the saddlebags over a shoulder, and went to look for a room. He found a vacancy at the Whitney House on Bridge Street. The room, numbered *214,* was on the second floor of the four-story building. It opened to a balcony that ran the width of the front, overlooking the street below. Downstairs, the first floor had a restaurant serving food 24 hours a day, and after settling in, he went down to eat.

The place was packed, and in the lobby, people stood waiting to be seated. Stryker stood in the doorway a moment, decided not to wait, and went looking for another restaurant.

Stryker walked down the main street on the opposite side from the train and depot. He came to an A-frame sidewalk sign which read, "The Best Beef Stew in Town. Take out." There was no line waiting to enter. He opened the door and stepped inside. The tables were small two-person size and all seven of them, were empty. The shop couldn't have been more than fifteen by fifteen feet and the counter in the rear took up some of that. He couldn't help wondering if he was the first customer of the day. No waiter in sight, Stryker slammed the door behind him and sat at the table farthest from the door. The tiny restaurant was squeezed between two larger buildings on either side, no windows. Not only were there no windows; there were no pictures on the walls, no flowers, and no coverings on tables. The place was bare bones. The only thing going for it was the boardwalk sign outside.

A waitress came from the kitchen behind the counter, early forties maybe, thin, dark hair, no smile. She wore a plaid shirt, denim slacks, and a furrowed brow, the kind one gets from constant worry. And, she looked awfully tired. She wasn't a bad looking woman, though. Without the scowl and tiredness, she would have been even more attractive. She took one look at Stryker and spun around to go back in the kitchen.

"Bring me a bowl of that stew," Stryker ordered, "and a beer."

She stopped, hesitated a moment, as if deciding what to do, and then turned to Stryker. "All right," she said, letting out a long breath, "I do have beer. It's warm."

Stryker sat with one arm resting on the table, looking implacable. "Is it always this crowded?"

"No." She acted as if she had more to say about it. Looking pensive, she firmed her mouth in a hard line. Instead, she let it go, and said, "I'll get the stew and beer." She whisked about and pushed through the swing door into the kitchen. A minute later, she burst out carrying a wooden bowl and a spoon in one hand, and a glass of beer in the other. She placed them both in front of Stryker without comment. She stood there, maybe expecting some sign of gratitude which never came. She gave up and turned to leave.

"I wanna talk to you," Stryker said. Steam rose from the bowl as he stirred the stew. His eyes were on the woman. "Sit down."

"I have nothing to say to you."

"Not who you think I am." Stryker reasoned from her comment, she suspected him to be someone bringing trouble.

"Who are you, then?" She made no move to sit.

"Name's Stryker. I want information." He loaded the spoon, blew on it, and tasted the stew. "Stew's good." He detected a slight melting of ice, but the woman remained standing. He ladled another spoon full. The lean beef, carrots, potatoes, tomatoes, and cabbage were spiced with pepper, salt, jalapeño, and beef stock. *Damn tasty, no problem finishing this bowl.*

"Information?" she asked, warily.

"The tavern by the lake–Tahoe–some woman ran it. Hear it burned down."

She stared at Stryker and said nothing. Maybe she was trying to decide. Maybe she didn't trust him, or maybe she didn't know what the hell he was talking about.

But her silence gave Stryker a notion she knew something about the place. "Think I'll ride over and take a look."

"Why?"

"How long you been open here?"

"A week."

Stryker let his eyes wander around the small, empty room. "Do much business?"

"You're the first. The stew and beer are 75 cents." With that, the woman turned and left Stryker alone to eat his meal.

He threw a silver dollar on the table when he finished eating.

The waitress known locally as Tahoe Tami peeped over the swing door and watched him leave.

Outside, his belly satisfied with the tasty stew, Stryker spied a saloon farther down the street and headed for it. He stopped after a few steps and turned around. No, he hadn't missed a sign. The tiny restaurant serving the best stew in town didn't have a name. The woman who serves the best stew in town didn't tell him her name either.

Truckee wasn't as raucous or dangerous as Bodie, but the town gave a good account of itself. Gunfights were held nightly, mostly from disputes in the red-light district on Jibboom Street, one street back of the town's main street, Donner Pass Road.

Disagreements in the plentiful saloons often ended in gunplay as well, but the chief cause of deadly shootouts emanated over the "rights" to sample the soiled doves. Loggers mostly, seeking female companionship after a hard day's work that included sawing and hauling logs used to build Virginia City, Sacramento, and San Francisco. They "squabbled" over their places in line. Truckee shouldn't be judged too harshly. "Squabbling" over a woman has been going on for a long time, and it even continues today! Something to do with nature, some say. It seems man "ain't" that far from animals in that regard. Besides, Truckee had few single women of "even proclaimed" virtue back then, so competition (squabbling) was fierce.

Stryker had given little thought about female companionship, but he wanted a cold beer. He'd gotten used to the chilled brews these days. Warm beer no longer seemed good enough. Miss No-Name should serve cold ones to go with the best stew in town. *Why no customers? Warm beer can't be the only reason.*

Stryker walked toward Harley's Saloon, on the same side of the street. Harley's, two doors down, was one of 28 saloons in Truckee. Evening brought a chill to the logging town, elevation 5,800 feet and lantern glow and piano music wafting out over the saloon's bat wings said "come on in." Truckee watering holes were all very much alike, an ornate bar with bottles of whiskey laced with dubious strychnine concoctions lined shelves behind the bartender, and round green felt tables were spaced around the room for gambling. Cigar and cigarette smoke drifted in layers over the room. A large group of men circled the faro table in the back and a smaller number of men played brag a little closer to the front. A roulette wheel had three men and two Painted Ladies by it in the corner. A piano opposite the bar had a man seated on a stool banging out lively tunes and seven or eight men were dancing with dance hall girls. Those girls weren't prostitutes. These women made more money dancing with the men than they'd make in bed. But fifty dances a night wore them out more than just lying on their backs. Behind the bar was a large mirror. Above that, a painting depicted a nude woman languidly resting on a brass bed. Bright cherry-red lips added color to the girl's pale white skin. Most watering holes had music, some had barber shops, and some had bordellos. But except for prostitutes and dance hall girls, women weren't allowed in saloons. Saloons offered camaraderie to men. The bartenders were among the most respected men in town, maybe because they held absolute reign, and their bar room supremacy often extended outside the saloon. It's possible the double-barreled shotguns kept under the counter added to their respectability.

A man standing across the street by the train depot watched Stryker enter Harley's. Then, a few minutes later, as Stryker leaned against the bar, sipping from a frosty mug, the watchful fellow slipped through the door and strode over to sit at a table with three other men. They exchanged greetings with eye contact or a nod, no talking. Loggers had soiled denims and woolen shirts, both worn and ragged. You could tell the four men at the table weren't loggers—nowhere near as filthy, no hobnail boots, and they didn't look all worn out from a day's work. They also wore sidearms.

"He was in Tami's for a while," the man said as he pulled out a chair. "Must have had a meeting."

"You sure it was a meeting, Mikhail?" One of the men asked. "Maybe he just went in to eat."

"Why don't you go ask him?" Mikhail retorted.

"I'll ask him." Another man at the table said, a nattily-dressed man who looked sure of himself.

"Sure, you go Kirill," Mikhail said. "We gotta tell Stanek somethin'." The men at the table spoke with thick east European accents.

Stryker was half finished with the beer when one of the four men rose and approached the bar. Stryker saw him coming in the mirror. He came up left of Stryker and ordered a beer.

"Haven't seen you around here before." Kirill shifted his body sideways and leaned on the counter, facing Stryker. He stood a little less than six feet, slight of build, hatless with curly black hair. Kirill leaned back, and he wore his mustache on a well-tanned face. He positioned himself where his gun and gun hand were not restricted by being next to the bar counter and hooked a thumb in his gun belt, two inches from the .44.

Stryker recognized the accent. It was the same as those Russian boys he'd met at West Point. He switched the beer to his left hand, stepped away from the bar, and swiveled to face Kirill.

Kirill then took in the full measure of Stryker's fierce countenance, grim mouth, a killer's icy pale eyes—cold and deadly, and how closely the stranger's gun hand hung by the Peacemaker.

The bartender slapped the beer on the counter. Kirill grabbed it and returned to his buddies around the table. They looked at him with questions scrolled on their faces.

"What's the matter, Kirill?" Mikhail asked. He and the other two men shifted their attention to Stryker.

"Nothing," Kirill said. He raised the mug and hastily sloshed down a mouthful of beer.

"Think we should tell Stanek?" Mikhail asked.

"We'll take care of him," Kirill groused, wiping foam from his face.

Stryker glanced in the mirror while he sipped beer. Each time he brought the mug to his mouth, he saw the four men at the table watching him. The mixed breed cut a striking figure and was used to the many stares, but the four men at the table looked like trouble.

Stryker placed the empty mug on the counter and shook his head no when the bartender asked if he wanted another.

"Say, mister, wanna a dance?" The thirties-something, bleached blond hauling around an extra twenty pounds, asked. Heavy on the makeup and soaked with a cheap imitation of Eau de Cologne, the saloon hussy held Stryker's elbow, entreating a dance with him. When Stryker turned and faced the woman, his looks shocked her. She started to walk away.

"Yes." Stryker had never danced a step in his life. He thought those people who liked to do the mating dance would be better off making use of those provocative moves in bed.

She spied him from across the ballroom floor. A brigade ball, Stryker outfitted in his dress blues, cut a handsome figure. Wearing the navy-blue jacket with polished brass buttons, a white shirt and black bow tie, royal blue slacks with red stripes for artillery, and sporting rows of medals and ribbons, his fierce some countenance fit–and somehow elevated his appearance to that of a dashing young officer.

Leigh, in her early twenties, with blond hair, blue eyes, and trim, erect figure approached him. "Dance with me, soldier," she'd said.

When they reached center floor, Stryker guided her outside to the veranda. They talked. Three hours later, he asked her to take his hand in marriage, and she said yes. That was the closest he'd ever come to dancing with a woman. Leigh knew he abhorred twinkled-toed sashaying, and she didn't want to see him flouncing about either. She never asked Stryker to dance again.

"Well, all right then. My name's Wanda." The slightly soiled dove took Stryker's hand without asking his name and led him between tables to an open floor space by the piano. No need to pull her close. She flattened her ample breasts against him and threw an arm around his neck. Being much taller than she, only her hand reached behind his neck. She grabbed his other hand, which was hanging by his side, and held it by her shoulder.

Tip-toeing up to Stryker's ear, she whispered, "Seventy-five cents for the dance." She attempted to lead off with a box step, and Stryker did his best not to stomp on her feet. He stumbled on every step, his size-twelve boots lurching from where they stuck on the floor to the next sticky placement. The woman's feet suffered an awful pounding.

"Looking for a woman called Tahoe Tami," Stryker said, leaning down closer. He asked her whereabouts, facing away from the four men watching them, and swung his partner around so they couldn't see her talk when she answered.

A puzzled frown crossed her brow, and she replied, "She ain't no dancer, mister. Besides, last I heard, she was in Tahoe City."

Stryker shuffled his clumsy feet a couple more times and stopped the crude waltz. He dug out a dollar gold piece from his front pocket and put it in her hand. After tipping the Stetson, an unusual courteous gesture for the mixed breed, he turned and walked out the bat-wings.

"What'd that man say to you, Wanda?" Kirill demanded. He waited until Stryker had gone and then leaped to his feet, stopping the dancer before she got another partner.

"He was looking for Tahoe Tami."

'Wha'd you tell 'im?"

"I said she was in Tahoe City." (Tahoe City was initially called "Tahoe." In 1949, it was officially changed to "Tahoe City." For clarity, that is what will be used for this story.)

A sly grin crossed Kirill's face. "You just saved yourself a good slapping, woman."

Outside Harley's, satisfied he'd gotten the information he wanted, Stryker headed back to the hotel to get a night's rest for an early start to Tahoe City the next morning. The tobacco smoke hadn't followed him out, but the raucous clamor accompanied him over the bat-wing doors. It died away as he walked up the street. He rounded the corner of Donner and Bridge Street and had just crossed Bridge when the door of the Whitney Hotel burst open and two young people rushed out, a boy and a girl, midteens. The boy carried what looked like a flour sack. The girl paused a half a second on the stoop and grabbed his arm.

"We're rich, Donnie!" The girl leaned close to kiss his cheek.

"Not now, Abby!" Donnie grabbed her hand and pulled her down the steps.

The double-barrel Greener blew its 210 shot-pattern through the front door's etched glass. Buckshot and glass fragments struck both teens above the shoulders. With the spinal cords laid bare to the base of their skulls, Donnie and Abby died before they landed face-first in the street. They lay in the mud with the boy still clutching the bag and holding the girl's hand. Inside the sack was eighty-seven dollars and forty-three cents.

Stryker side-stepped to his right and waited. The shotgun could have been re-loaded.

"I don't know if I just meant to scare 'em or kill 'em," the hotel owner said, peering through the shattered glass. He opened the door. More glass fell out onto the wooden planks and made scrunching sounds under his boots as he came out to stand on the stoop. He looked down at the two bodies. "I guess I meant to kill 'em."

"Reckon so," Stryker allowed. He walked around the slain teens, climbed the steps, and entered the hotel. He left the shotgun-toting hotelier standing on the stoop. The crumpled *Examiner* lay on the counter next to the clerk's sign-in register. Stryker figured he wouldn't be the first person to read it. Fair enough, then. He'd be the last. He stuffed the newspaper under his arm and climbed the stairs to the second floor. He'd napped on the train, but he wanted a good night's sleep before starting out for the long ride to Tahoe City. Reading the paper in bed might make the eyelids heavier. He saw nothing in the personals for him.

"Where do I get on the trail to Tahoe City?" Stryker asked the hotel clerk the next morning–the same one as the night before. Stryker leaned his back against the chest-high desk and eyed the front doors. The remaining glass had been removed. Dawn was ushering in a gray light. He turned back to the clerk and put three dollars, the agreed upon cost of the night's lodging, on the counter.

"Go back up the street along the tracks and the river, then follow the stage road along the river to the lake, could be sixteen miles or more." The desk clerk pointed to a spacious arched doorway. "Breakfast in there, it's included with the room."

The killings from the night before weren't mentioned. Later, when Stryker dropped down the front steps, he noticed the blood had been covered up with sawdust. Two lives, two young lives, now covered over with sawdust. "Eighty-seven dollars and forty-three cents. They were rich for about half a minute," Stryker grumbled. "Stupid shits."

The horse, which Stryker never bothered to name, nickered a greeting when he entered its stall. Fifteen minutes later, he led the roan outside and climbed into the saddle. He rode west up the street, passing the Central Pacific resting on tracks between him and the river. Its engine blew huge billows of steam as if it were out of breath from crossing the Sierra's. Quiet morning ride through town, it was still early enough to where few people were out. Those who were, kept to themselves. Whether it was the morning chill or because they weren't fully reconciled with the start of a workday, no one was friendly. Nor was Stryker, although he might have tipped his Stetson to a good-looking woman, if he saw one.

Stryker came upon the stage road about a half mile west of downtown Truckee. Heading south toward the lake, it bridged the Truckee River. Being a well-traveled road, it was wide enough for two stagecoaches to pass one another. The trail ran off the right of the river and after about four or five miles; he saw cut logs floating downstream, which meant logging crews up ahead had begun their workday. Sugar pine, Jeffery pine, fir, and aspen trees grew heavily along the steep slopes. Many of the mature sugar pines had already been cut, leaving mostly smaller Sugars growing on the mountainsides rising from the river. Suppling lumber for Virginia City mines and San Francisco's building boom had decimated the forest around Lake Tahoe in the late 1800s. Fortunately, the forest recovered.

Stryker reined the roan at a wide intersection with a sign that read "Squaw Valley Road." The road ran westward into a broad grassy valley. Bear Creek wound its way through the lush meadows of the valley and emptied into the Truckee River. Stryker dismounted and led the roan to the creek's icy mountain water. A stagecoach and a Gypsy wagon had also pulled over to water their horses, although now the stage was turning back away from the creek and back on the road to Tahoe City. The Gypsy driver, a woman, was leading two horses to the creek when Stryker and the roan turned off to rest. From his fractured view of the woman, Stryker figured she could have been anywhere from her midthirties to late forties. Hard to tell. She had a look about her which said she'd lived a harsh life. A well-tanned, weathered face with worried lines, she was a thin thing, but it didn't appear hers was a life of leisure. She wore a black skirt, full and free flowing. Frayed at the bottom, it draped over the tops of her boots. A brown leather vest covered all but the long sleeves of a purple satin shirt. A wide black leather belt with a bold brass buckle was worn about her narrow waist. A red silk scarf was wrapped about her head like a bandanna. At one point in the woman's life, Stryker mused to himself, she could have been quite fetching.

Another female, a younger woman, sat on the wagon's footboard. Gypsy drivers sat on the footboard, dangling their feet below, or resting them on the cross board of the harness shafts. The front opening of the Gypsy wagon is used as a regular doorway. A customary buckboard bench would make getting in and out of the wagon cumbersome. This colorful wagon had the customary rounded roof. It was painted a very shiny purple, and the rest of the wagon was bright red except for an array of stemmed roses above the side window. The roses were painted black, and they resembled eyelashes over the round window. A smokestack protruded from the purple roof. Stryker had seen Gypsy wagons before, but none as colorful as this one. The girl on the wagon was very pretty.

He brought the roan to the creek, next to the Gypsy's horses. The roan and the Gypsy horses were between Stryker and the woman while the animals drank. Words were not exchanged. With a command and a sharp tug on the halters, she pulled her horses from the stream. Stryker waited a while longer, allowing the roan to munch on the tall grass prior to mounting up. She had almost finished harnessing her horses to the Gypsy wagon when he rode by. The girl on the seat gave him a bashful smile. She whirled about and slipped through the door before Stryker could assess her age, though he guessed less than eighteen. The Gypsy woman busied herself with the harnessing–looking a little too busy doing it. She didn't look up to acknowledge the mixed breed. He pulled right on the reins, pressed his left knee on the roan's withers, and turned south on the road toward Tahoe City.

A little farther up, the road crossed the river. The wooden bridge led the road upside the left of the river now. Stryker rode easy in the saddle, taking in the natural beauty of the valley and the mountains that stretched up from the river. The water flowed peaceful and tranquil in long lazy ribbons interrupted by short spats where it grew angry and rushed along in white-capped rapids.

Stryker rounded a sharp bend on a steep upgrade. Rapids chased the drop in elevation. Seemingly out of place, intermittent booms sounding like distant thunder punctuated the roar of rushing water, and they grew louder as he rode up the road. A little beyond the rapids, he soon discovered the source of the booming. Stryker had seen log skids and log flumes in the Big Basin tree cuts near Felton, California, but this was the first time he'd seen a dry log chute. Logs in water flumes floated comfortably along a lazy river, usually reaching speeds no more than ten miles an hour. Dry chutes instead of water flumes were used on the steep slopes around Tahoe. Loggers greased the waterless chutes with tallow to aid the logs on their way to the river. And did they slide! Thirty-foot sugar pines reached speeds of seventy miles an hour hurtling down the mountainside. The big logs had even been timed, flashing down a half mile section of a chute in five seconds! Of course, not all the logs remained in the lightning-fast chutes all the way to the water. Often a log would leap from the chute and pinwheel down the mountain. But even if a log made it to the river in the wooden trough, the entrance was anything but a graceful dive into the receiving pool. When a log hit, water exploded skyward in huge hundred-foot sprays. Sometimes a log landed on logs already floating in the pool and would bounce across the river to impale half its length in the opposite bank. Logging along the Truckee was exciting–and dangerous work.

Chutes on trestles crossed over the road, allowing people on horses and wagons to travel under the sliding logs. A watchful traveler, one who knew about the dangers of logs hopping out of the chutes, would gauge spaces between them, and then hurriedly pass under the trestles.

Stryker, unfamiliar with dry chutes, failed to expect an errant log from the far side of the river to bounce over the river and fly across the road. He was surveying the road ahead and failed to see the thirty-foot log pin-wheeling toward him. It clipped his head and a clip by a five-ton log was all it took to damn near kill him.

CHAPTER SEVEN

Stryker heard two women talking. They were discussing what to put in the stew. "Onions, potatoes, tomatoes," one of them said, and the other woman, sounding older, opined it was the last time they could use the duck neck and the damn thing needed all the help it could get. They spoke as if they were the only two people there. Stryker wondered if they were.

He listened to the women and tried to make sense of things as he struggled to open his eyes. *Why won't they open? The women talking, were they the Gypsies?* He attempted to speak. Someone glued his mouth together and whatever words he intended to say came out as a weak moan.

"What was that?" The older woman looked toward the bed where Stryker lay.

"What was what, Dya?"

"Go see about him, Vienna. I'll finish the stew."

The Gypsy wagon, true to its style, was like a small apartment on wheels with beds or bunks in the rear, a tiny living room space, storage cabinets, and a compact kitchen plus stove—all very colorful. Stryker lay on the most rearward bunk. It was situated crossways and elevated off the floor with a set of four drawers underneath. Two more elevated bunks, smaller, were along the side walls perpendicular to the bunk on which he lay.

Vienna lit a candle and shielded it with a cupped hand as she moved to the back of the wagon. Apprehension and curiosity accompanied her. If Stryker regained consciousness, would he be a danger? What would he be like? "Major?" She whispered. No response. She called out louder, "Major?" A quick head jerk and Stryker scrunched his face looking confused. His eyes remained shut.

"Dya. Mother, I think he's trying to wake up!" Using her free hand, Vienna nudged Stryker's shoulder.

"Lemme' see." The Gypsy mother dropped a wooden spoon and wiped her hands on her apron as she scurried to Stryker's bunk.

Stryker lifted his eyebrows in a vain attempt to unglue the sticky eyelids. He canted his head toward the candlelight.

"Major, if you can hear me, nod your head. Hold the candle a little closer, Vienna."

The request was almost imperceptible, but Stryker's chin did dip.

"Dya!" Vienna whispered excitedly. "He heard you!"

"Mister, I'm Nadya. My daughter here is Vienna" Nadya laid the back of her hand against Stryker's cheek. "He's not as hot. Maybe, this time it'll hold."

"What day is it?" Stryker asked, his eyes staying closed.

"Dya!" Vienna gasped, and she grabbed her mother's arm.

"Friday," Nadya said. "Get a warm washcloth, that one by the bowl." She pointed at the wet hand cloth hanging off a metal washbasin. "It's on the cabinet there—quickly, Vienna."

Vienna ran to the washbowl and came back with the cloth. "It's still a little warm."

Nadya took the cloth and began gently applying it to Stryker's eyes, moistening the eyelids, and wiping away the sleep gunk. "Blink your eyes several times."

Squinting and blinking, Stryker looked up at the two women. "I've been out for four days?"

"Six weeks, mister—month and a half," Nadya said. She spoke sternly, as if to leave no doubt or brook any questions.

Stryker stared at Nadya, trying to comprehend what she'd just told him.

"You've lost weight, and you're weak," Nadya warned. "Don't try to get up yet. We kept you alive on broth and water. Thought you would die. You're a tough man, but you'll have to take it slow. Got to regain strength and it'll take time. Stomach shrunk."

"Why?" Stryker asked, clearing his throat.

"Why'd we save you?" Nadya replied.

Dya's a doctor," Vienna said. "You're her patient."

Stryker looked past the women and at the Gypsy wagon's interior.

"It's a long story. Tell you later," Nadya said.

Stryker moved his hands under the covers, feeling his body as far down as he could reach without bending. His hand felt the edge of something around his upper right leg.

"Yes, you're naked," Nadya said, noticing his exploring hands. "You broke your right tibia. It's set in plaster-of-Paris. We stripped you looking for other fractures. You also had to be cleaned daily and cleaning included bodily evacuations."

"You're lucky Dya knew how to set and bind your leg with the plaster," Vienna said. "Most doctors still use wood and leather."

"By the time you regain enough strength to stand, the leg should be healed." Nadya said, turning to Vienna. "Bring some broth." Back to Stryker, "I figured you weighed close to two hundred pounds when we managed to get you in the wagon. You're good fifty pounds lighter now. You'll need to eat, but we'll have to go slow, like I said. It's a miracle you're alive."

"We prayed for you every day," Vienna added.

Stryker pulled an arm from under the blanket. Holding it up, he looked at it. Perhaps trying to prove it had been six weeks. Skin hung from the bones in wrinkled, shapeless strips. For the first time in his life, he felt true fear. Though his life had hung on a razor's edge before, he'd always prevailed with gun, blade, or guile by his own efforts. Here he was helpless, depending on someone else–these two women. And he'd learned they'd prayed for him too–for a miracle. *He and God had always left each other alone.* He'd repeated that more than once when asked about religion. Now he reconsidered. "I reckon your prayers were answered."

Three days later, Nadya cut the cast off his leg. Stryker took one look at the emaciated appendage and winced.

"Don't worry, it'll grow back," Nadya said.

It was two weeks before Stryker could stand, and then he had to be supported by the women on either side. They massaged his legs and gradually applied resistance, pushing or pulling on his feet to work the muscles. During that time, he learned more about Doctor Strickler. She insisted he call her Nadya. Before medical school in Philadelphia, she'd married Samuel Strickler, a lawyer, and had their daughter, Vienna. The three of them moved to Saint Louis, Missouri after she got her license to practice. A couple years passed and a cholera epidemic hit. Her first three patients died. Her male counterpart in town fared better. He'd referred the sickest patients to her. Female doctors were almost unheard of, and their competency was constantly being questioned. There was even talk of witchery. Her husband came down with the disease as one of the three. He refused treatment from the male doctor, insisting his wife could save him. She couldn't. When she failed to even save her own husband, things got a lot worse. Relatives of the other two deceased patients vowed to avenge their deaths. One of them was a wealthy owner of a successful brewery and he vowed to kill Nadya and Vienna. A friend came to warn their lives were in danger and they escaped from town in the middle of the night. They met an enclave of Gypsies, camped ten miles west of Saint Louis, and traded their buggy for a Gypsy wagon. The gypsies demanded more in trade and Nadya treated a ten-year-old boy with an injured hand that had been crushed by a wagon wheel. She also gave them forty dollars, and they promised not to reveal anything about Nadya and Vienna, names they'd now given themselves to pass as Gypsies.

They found clothing left in the wagon and put it on, thinking a disguise might protect them from being recognized. They didn't want to chance a traveler to Saint Louis telling folks he'd seen the two women. Were they being followed by angry mob members and what would they do to them if they were caught? The masquerade worked so well; they continued to wear Gypsy garb and traveled west, heading for California.

Nadya drove the wagon and Vienna remained inside. Nadya made up their faces to look as though they might be sick with the pox. People left them alone.

"We heard about the lake in Truckee," Vienna sitting by his bed told Stryker. "We'd been here a week before we came upon you on the way back from Truckee. It's even more beautiful than we heard. I think Dya wasn't all that upset to stay for a while. We didn't think it would be this long, though." She smiled, as if to imply although he'd been an inconvenience, they didn't mind all that much. "We made a little money telling fortunes and treating injured loggers with Gypsy medicine. The idiots felt more confidant with a conjure woman than a female doctor."

"I'd like to see it," Stryker said.

"See what?" Nadya asked, climbing into the wagon. Stryker and Vienna watched her place a burlap sack on the table.

"The lake Dya, he's never seen it. At least I don't think he has. You haven't, have you?" Vienna asked.

"No." Stryker wondered if Nadya had brought groceries from a nearby town. "We're near a town?"

"Tahoe City," Nadya said, pulling vegetables, fruits, and a salted ham wrapped in wax paper from the sack. "We're about three miles south of it."

"By the lake," Vienna added.

"You need to get fresh air," Nadya said. "You feel up to getting out of the wagon?"

"Reckon so, with a little help." Stryker hated to admit it, but he would still need them helping him.

"Tomorrow then," Nadya said. "Get a good night's sleep."

The next morning, after a breakfast of sliced ham, berries, and dates, the women helped Stryker leave the bed where he'd spent weeks. He had to lean on them to cross the wagon floor to its front. If he had looked in a mirror, he would have seen a stick man with clothes hanging on him. "I must sit for a minute," he groaned. He slumped to the driver's bench. "Damn it, I'm a pathetic excuse for a man."

"You are pathetically weak, no good to yourself or anyone else," Nadya agreed.

"I deserved that," Stryker said, swinging his feet around. There would be no more self-pity, and he silently admonished himself for the moment of weakness. "Let's go look at the lake."

On unsteady legs, and with the women holding him, Stryker managed to walk the one-hundred feet to the shoreline. They guided him to a round granite boulder, the one Nadya and Vienna had sat on many mornings to take in the lake's view. Stryker allowed them to guide his rump onto the rock. Recollections of Leigh, his dead wife, or Morgan and the Hearst job, subject matters which had recently occupied much of his waking hours, faded away as he sat and enjoyed Lake Tahoe's splendor.

Across the azure water, mountains rose over 10,000 feet surrounding the lake. Peaks of which were caped in brilliant white snow, silhouetted against a blue sky that was broken up with only a few white, billowy clouds. Closer in, the shallow water became clear turquoise where smooth granite boulders, like the one he sat on, dotted the shoreline. Nature, he thought, can produce a beauty no artist can fully capture, and it was no mystery why Nadya and Vienna interrupted their trip to California to spend time by the lake… and save his life.

He spied a girl, maybe seven- or eight-years old, running and laughing along the beach with her little dog yapping excitedly beside her. He didn't see her parents, so he just watched the girl and dog. "I can see why you stayed here. I'm a little relieved it wasn't entirely because of me."

Nadya and Vienna replied with smiles, not at him though, but at the panoramic view before them.

"As soon as I'm able, I have a job to do here and in Truckee," Stryker sounding somewhat resigned to his task ahead. "If you can give me a week after I leave here, I'd like to come back and travel with you to California."

"Are you a wanted man?" Nadya asked. "I'd like to know if we should regret saving your *sorry* ass." She pounded Stryker again for his self-pity comment.

"I killed a man most responsible for my wife's death."

"Murder? You're wanted for his murder?"

"Yes."

Nadya thought a minute and then asked, "What about the other person? You said *most* responsible. You kill him too? Who was he?"

Stryker drew in a deep breath. He paused and then exhaled the weighty reply. "Me," He said, watching the girl and dog.

Nadya glanced at Vienna. "Well, let's not talk any more about that."

"Stryker, when we first saw you watering your horse at Squaw Road, we were frightened you'd been sent after us from Saint Louis," Nadya began. "You rode on ahead, though. Still, we were concerned you might lie in wait to ambush us. Frankly, we had doubts for a long time."

Stryker turned to Nadya. "And you saved my life, anyway."

Gradually, Stryker's appetite returned and, along with it, his strength. He walked on his own and did exercises to build up his muscles. He did little chores around the wagon camp and helped where he could. He gained back half his lost weight in less than a month.

"I'll be leaving tomorrow," he announced after another week. I'll be back in a few days. When I do, I'll take you to San Francisco. Wait for me."

The following morning, he strapped on his gun belt, taking up two extra notches. He took the sai and stuffed it in the leather holster at the small of his back. The women watched him as he readied himself in the wagon.

"What's that you put behind your back?" Vienna asked.

"Weapon. Comes in handy."

"Oh," was all Vienna had to say, apparently choosing not to pursue the sai's deadly purpose.

Stryker threw on the Stetson. Even that felt loose. "Before I go, tell me your real names."

"June. My daughter, Sarah."

All right June, wait for me." Stryker said, climbing down from the wagon.

Outside, Stryker thought he may have been too hasty. He struggled with putting the halter, saddle, and cinch on the roan. When he finally got into the saddle, he was puffing hard. But he'd committed to leave, and he started riding north.

June and Sarah stood by the Gypsy wagon and watched as he rode up a hill and out of sight. "Are we gonna wait, mother?"

"Yes."

When Stryker arrived in Tahoe City and asked four people, a grocer, a blacksmith, a saloonkeeper, and an old woman at a boarding house about Tahoe Tami, all of them said she had gone to Truckee four months ago. Four to one. Wanda lied to him. Why?

Finally, after riding the five miles to Squaw Creek Road, Stryker was compelled to stop and rest. He lay by the creek and dozed while the roan munched on lush grass nearby.

A half hour later, Stryker awoke, realizing where he was and why he'd had to rest. He looked up at the blue sky and watched a single white cloud float lazily behind the forested hill across the Truckee River. He sat up, taking a few extra minutes before getting to his feet. A bug, a little red one, was slowly working its way up the denim on his leg. Being no entomologist, or even a *bugologist*, he nevertheless recognized the small insect as a Lady Bug. He pressed the fingernail on his middle finger against his thumb to flip it off. Then he hesitated, and began to marvel at the small insect, as it worked its way back and forth on his pant leg. *Random evolvement? What evolution led to bugs? This bug. For that matter, how or why did all earth's creatures come about? Could it be by design and with a purpose?* He chided himself. Silly of him to think about such weighty subjects, he reasoned. It was just a stupid bug. But why was his life spared? Was there a purpose for that? Throughout his whole life it seemed as though he'd met only tragedy, hardship, and evil, the only exception being briefly with his wife, Leigh, and now Morgan. He had no real friends. Leigh became a tragedy and Morgan started out as a business arrangement and never seemed to go much beyond that, even though there was great temptation on both sides. He wouldn't let it, the *damned jinx* would have killed her, so he kept his distance from Morgan. Now strangers rescued him, June, and Sarah. He'd never encountered good people like them before, and they were *good* people. They'd done much to keep him alive and he couldn't help wondering if there was a purpose somehow mixed in with that. *Purpose, that word again.* Regardless, he owed the women, and he would have to pay them back, part of his code. The Lady Bug had just about worked its way up to his pocket now. He tore off a leafy weed and held it in front for the insect to crawl on. Stryker sat the leaf on the ground and the little bugger scrambled away in the tall grass.

Stryker mused to himself–*has that bug just changed my life*? He got to his feet. Then it was even harder to mount the roan, and he had to bring the big horse beside a stump to help him climb in the saddle. The introspection wouldn't leave him alone, though. He'd never been given to this kind of self-examination. He'd always thought he was alive and one day he wouldn't be. Somewhere down the road, a bullet would be quicker than his and that would end it. Now it seemed as if there was more to it than that. Maybe his life had meaning, but what kind? *This is crazy,* he thought. His weakened condition was making him think this way. *Crazy, yeah,* but was there some good in him he had yet to do? June and Sarah–helping June get a medical practice established in San Francisco somehow did not seem enough. Was there something else? Should he now look upon life with a different perspective, that being simply killing anyone who crossed him? These thoughts tugged on him as he rode toward Truckee. Organized religion had never played a part in his life, and it didn't enter his consciousness now. But an emerging force, whether emanating from within him or from an outside mysterious source, was too intense to ignore. He tried to concentrate on the task at hand, finding Tahoe Tami, doing whatever it took to make Hearst feel he'd helped a woman he obviously still cared for. The job would most likely require his unique skills with gun and blade, perhaps all of them, and he couldn't allow his mind, his focus, to wander. But the nagging query about his own life's direction kept creeping back into his head.

Leaning against the roan's neck for much of the ride to Truckee, he ignored the river, the landscape's beauty, and everything else until reaching town. Then he ignored the men stacking logs, the angry puffing of a locomotive that had just rolled in, and the people who stared at him as he rode past. Exhausted as he was, he straightened in the saddle down Donner Pass Street to the Whitney House. There, the desk clerk informed him he had no one to take the roan to the stable. Sam's blacksmith and livery, which he'd used two and a half months ago, was farther east along Church Street behind Whitney's, and opposite a plaza. The only other stable was at the west end of town. It used to be the largest building in Truckee. Hotels which had sprung up after the fires of 1873, 1875, and 1878 were larger now. Sam's, although much smaller than its west-end competitor, captured travelers arriving from the east. It was a short walk two and a half months ago. It seemed much longer to the weary man today. He led the roan down the street and across the plaza. The heavy sliding door hung closed. Too early in the day for it.

He'd only slid the heavy wooden door open a few inches when he heard the wail of a man in pain from inside. Stryker shoved the door open farther and led the roan into the livery. He'd only gone a few steps when he heard another man growl a throaty demand. "Tell us dammit, or I'll lay the whole shoe on you!"

"Please, I ain't got it here."

"Where? Then."

"The bank. I went there this morning!"

Stryker tied the roan to a stall post and crept quietly on down the center aisle with the Peacemaker drawn. The back door was closed as well, and the rear of the livery was dark. But in the left corner, he saw the shadows of two men standing in the forge's glow. Horses gave low nickers as he passed their stalls. Like all liveries, this one had the stench of horse shit and piss, but Stryker thought he smelled something else, like maybe the pungent odor of burning flesh.

"Your lying! The bank ain't open yet. Now, Pete, where the hell is it?"

"Hit him again, Jessie."

"You wanna do it, Regis" Jessie yelled at the taller man. Regis just shrugged his shoulders and said nothing. Jessie turned his attention back to the blacksmith. "I ain't gonna kill you, yet anyway, but you're gonna tell where you hid the gold!" Holding a glowing red horseshoe in a set of tongs, he jammed the two ends in the blacksmith's chest again.

"Ahhhh!"

Stryker cocked the Peacemaker. The angry shouting stifled the sound. He slipped close to an open stall near the forge. The two men standing had their backs to him. Stryker couldn't see the men's faces, but by their well-worn clothing, he guessed they could have been loggers or down-and-out miners. Being gruff with the blacksmith was no act. It appeared they planned to kill him unless they got what they wanted. The third man, Pete, sat on the floor facing the two men standing over him. Ropes tied around his belly and neck secured him against the anvil. His leather apron was pulled down and his shirt lay open. Two sets of bloody welts, each four inches apart, stuck out from his hairy chest from where the hot horseshoe had burned into his flesh. One man stood a half head taller than his partner. The shorter man, Stryker figured, was the one called Jessie, held the horseshoe in the tongs.

Stryker figured the scene for what it appeared, robbery attempt. Jessie heated the horseshoe in the fire again, shifted the grip, turned, and flattened it against the blacksmith's chest.

"Ahhhh–God!" Pete cursed the men through gritted teeth. "Damn you bastards!"

Stryker fired the Colt. The heavy slug smacked Jessie's back and he forward on the tortured blacksmith. The tongs and horseshoe fell to the dirt floor.

Regis whirled and groped for his sidearm. Stryker killed him with a bullet in his chest, left of center, before he could get the pistol out of his holster.

"Thank God you showed up, mister," Pete grunted from under the first man shot. "Get him off and untie me. Shit-damn this hurts," he groaned.

Stryker grabbed Jessie's collar and rolled him off the blacksmith.

Only he wasn't dead yet. His eyes were open, and he looked up at

Stryker. "The son-of- bitch stole our gold." Those were his last words and then he died.

Stryker pulled back the hammer on the Peacemaker and shoved its barrel against the blacksmith's forehead. "Where's the gold?"

"In that box." The blacksmith started to nod, but Stryker pressed the gun barrel too snug against him, so he pointed with his eyes at a green metal toolbox. It was two-by-three-by-two, closed with an iron lock on it, and sitting in the corner of the forge. "I'll give you half."

The Colt roared a third time. Stryker stabled the roan and walked out of the livery. Rounding up a ball of saliva in his mouth, he turned his head to spit. *Some fucking do-gooder I turned out to be.* He left the box untouched.

The adrenaline from the killings served to temporarily revive him, but by the time he climbed up the steps to the hotel, his strength was almost gone.

After paying for room *310* on the third floor–nothing being available on lower levels–the aroma of sizzling steaks lured him to the dining room before climbing the two flights of stairs.

He entered from the lobby and selected a table by the window. Being prior to 5 o'clock, twelve tables out of eighteen remained vacant. There was only the one window. It looked out onto the street. The side wall opposite the doorway from the lobby didn't have a window and the pale green wainscot was bare except for a hanging picture of an old man and woman, maybe the owners, or the original owners. A swing door led to the kitchen. The tables were covered with food-stained red and white checkered tablecloths, but each did have clean white linen napkins, four per sitting, three on Stryker's table by the window. Other diners paid no attention to Stryker's entrance and continued exchanging words in inaudible murmurs. He ordered a meal from a plump waitress with cropped, graying hair. She took his order and repeated it back to him to ensure its accuracy. Showing irksome nervousness, her voice quivered as she spoke. Even though Stryker looked somewhat emaciated, his facial features could still make people nervous.

Pearl, at least that's what her name tag said, brought the steak, pota-toes, and green beans, and a cold mug of beer twenty minutes later. The beer was topped with a two-inch foam head and Stryker sipped it, being careful not to get froth on his upper lip. It wasn't a particularly good brew, but it had been over two months since he'd had a cold one. The steak was a first in over two months as well. He cut into the medium rare steak, which was still very hot, and its enticing flavor tickled his nose before the first bite made it to his mouth. The food tasted delicious, the beer, the meat, the mashed potatoes, and beans, and he had to force himself to take enough time to enjoy his supper.

When he'd finished eating the last bite, he paid for the meal and headed up the stairs with renewed energy. At least it felt like he had more vivacity. At the top of the stairs leading to the third floor, he was puffing hard. *Not there yet,* he had to admit. Down the hall, he spied a sign protruding from the wall over a door that read *toilet and bath.* A hot, or even warm, bath sounded damn good. It was still relatively early in the evening, and he might be among the first to bathe in the tub. After the hot bath–he was the first one that night to use it–he returned to room *312.* He turned the doorknob, went inside, and fell on a bed, taking off only his gun belt and boots. There was a bed by each of the side walls, a small writing desk with a simple straight-back chair sat by the window. The window had no curtains. None of it mattered to him. He didn't notice the setting sun throwing streaks of light through the window, and in those rays, he didn't see floating dust particles either. Stryker was bushed.

The following morning, very early just after sunup, a knock on the door and female voice announcing "housekeeping" woke Stryker from another fitful dream. He couldn't decide whether to be annoyed or grateful.

"Come in." He swung his feet to the floor and started working them into his boots.

In walked the maid, carrying towels and sheets. The hotel was the only one in town providing fresh washcloths, towels, and linens. Stryker recognized her as the waitress he'd met on his first night in Truckee. It was only after he saw the name tag on her light-gray uniform with white collars that told him her name.

"Tami, Tahoe Tami." Stryker said. "Would've saved me a shit-load of trouble if I'd known your damn name before I rode out."

"I'll leave these here and come back later." Tami dumped the towels and bedding on the un-used bed. She heard the door slam behind her, and she snapped around to see Stryker blocking her way out of the room. She backed away until her legs hit the bed frame and she fell backward to sit on the mattress. Frightened of the fierce-looking man, she curled back against the wall.

"Let's you and me have a talk," Stryker growled.

"Who are you?" Tami's voice trembled. "What do you want?" She looked afraid, as if she thought Stryker might rape or kill her, or both.

"Information."

"Information? That's it?"

Stryker nodded.

"Okay," Tami said. She sat up.

"Tell me about your places shut down."

"You know about that?" She asked, sounding surprised.

"Not enough. Tell me." *What the hell did she think I wanted?*

"Two taverns with rooms to let, a saloon, and the café where you ate."

"All closed," Stryker said.

"Yes, the taverns and saloon were burned down, and they put a sign on the café door saying it was quarantined. I took it down twice. There was a threatening note the third time. Said I'd be sorry if I took it down again."

Stryker, keeping a watchful eye on Tami in case she bolted for the door, stepped over and grabbed the chairback. He twirled it around, sat with its back in front, and rested his forearms arms on top. "And you don't know who did it."

"No. I'm the only woman with saloons an' such. I guess they didn't like that." Tami crossed her legs and leaned forward. "Now, who are you?"

"Here to help you."

Tami straightened. "Help me, why?"

"Been hired."

"Hired? By whom?"

"Can't tell you."

"Someone here? Brought you in?"

"See anyone start the fires? Anyone looking suspicious?"

"No, never," Tami huffed, apparently resigned she would not learn the name of the mystery person, not yet, anyway. "You look awfully thin."

"You have friends here," Stryker said, a question in a statement.

"Not really. All who worked for me left after the last fire. There's Dud, that's all. He works here part time. The hotel hired me to take his place, 'cause he can't keep up anymore. Got too old. "What happened to you?" Concern showed on her face. It almost looked genuine.

"Logging accident."

"You don't look like a logger." She softened a bit. Then she eyed the Peacemaker and sai and returned to serious.

"I want to talk to Dud," Stryker said.

"What for? He won't know anything."

Stryker glared at her, waiting for an answer.

"He has a small room on the ground floor. Used to be a storage unit next to the kitchen. When they built a larger room behind the kitchen for extra storage, they let him stay in the old one. He's worked for Mister Mckay for a long time, I suppose. He owns the place. He's the man who hired me."

"I want to talk to him, too." Stryker got to his feet and shoved the chair to the desk with his foot. "You can go."

Tami, acting surprised, slipped off the bed and turned to pick up the towels and bedding.

"Leave 'em. Come back later. Keep your job at the hotel so I can find you." Stryker gave the orders, short, clipped, and direct, like military commands. He wasn't feeling all that well. Questions weren't tolerated.

"If you're gonna kill the man who's been burning me out, ask him why before you kill him." Tami scooted out the door. She carefully eased it behind her.

Stryker finished getting dressed, which meant he strapped on the gun belt and sai. Investigation would wait until after a breakfast of steak and eggs, and black coffee. Maybe that would help him regain strength, put weight on himself, and people wouldn't ask questions about his health. He hated explaining his damn frailty.

He finished breakfast and walked down a hallway to where he figured was Dud's room. He banged a fist on the door. The door appeared to have been recently installed because the paint didn't match, and Stryker figured this new entrance was for Dud's private use. It allowed him to enter and leave from the hallway and not have to go through the kitchen.

The door cracked open an inch. "Hello?" The man remained hidden behind the door.

Stryker jammed the point of his boot in the cracked opening and stuck the envelope Hearst had given him through the cracked opening.

There was a moment's pause, and then, "What do you want?"

"Information," Stryker said. The bottom of the door pressed against his boot. "Open the damn door." Stryker braced his shoulder against the door and shoved it open.

Fortunately, Dud had stepped back and wasn't knocked to the floor. "I figured you'd break it down," he said.

Stryker came in and looked around Dud's room. It was very small and very sparse. Being a former storeroom, there were no windows. A double bed, wooden table the size of a writing desk, and a single chair to go with it, and shelving left over from its use as a storage pantry, completed the furniture. Two faded black and white photographs of who Stryker guessed was of Dud's family sat on one of the shelves. The rest of the shelving on that wall held canned goods, dishes, and cookware. The other walls were filled with folded clothing. By the kitchen door was a wooden steamer chest secured with two brass straps running atop the curved lid and down the sides, suggesting Dud may have been at sea at one time. An envelope on the table was addressed to Dudley Marbridge, care of the Whitney House, Truckee, California.

Dud, limping badly with one leg shorter than the other, had led Stryker into the room. His shoulders slumped forward, and he was probably four inches taller when he was younger, that is, before the stooped posture and the shortened leg. A thin man, he looked as though he'd worked hard his whole life and maybe that had kept the weight off. He turned and plopped on the bed with a groan. "Have a seat," he said, pointing a rough and cracked hand at the wooden chair. The old man's white hair had grown yellow from lack of regular washing. A weathered history was etched on his sun-burned, craggy face. Dud pulled the makings from his shirt pocket and opened the drawstring on the little cloth pouch. He put his forefinger in one end of the paper fold with his thumb underneath and sprinkled tobacco onto rolling paper. After licking an edge, he rolled the paper together, and then rotated the roll in his fingers to get the lumps out of the tobacco. He lit one end of the cigarette, inhaled a long draw, and held it in a moment before blowing the smoke out. "Where'd you get the letter, mister?"

"Why'd you send it?" Stryker asked.

You could tell Dud was wrestling with whether or not he could trust Stryker. He took a gamble. "The girl needed help. Thought they might kill her."

"She a friend of yours?"

"No, and she has no idea I wrote to help her. We ain't got many women in Truckee–other than the whores."

"Who's doing it?"

"Don't have a clue," Dud answered with a grin, visibly relieved about Stryker now. "You got a name?"

"Stryker." He said, pulling out the desk chair and taking a seat. Never saw her threatened," Stryker asked in a statement.

"No. I never spent much time with the woman."

"The taverns and saloon. Where were they?" Stryker asked in a proper question.

"All I know is what I heard. The first one, I was told, was across the lake by the incline. Sierra Nevada Lumber company used an incline railway to haul logs up an' over the mountain. They needed timber for the Comstock, and they flumed them down the other side." Dud rubbed his chin. "I reckon that don't much matter to you though, but they opened a post office in '82 and Tami built a tavern for the loggers sometime after that." Dud became more talkative.

"Many taverns around there?"

"Only one as far as I know, 'nother one ain't opened neither."

"The second tavern," Stryker said.

"Torched in Tahoe City."

"Same lumber company in Tahoe City," Stryker asked in an irritating monotone.

"No, different outfit," Dud said. "And the saloon was here in Truckee. I wrote Hearst after that one. So, I figure the woman was in real trouble. Somebody was out to put her out of business or maybe kill her. They got over twenty saloons in town, I reckon, and they burned just hers."

"And shut down the café," Stryker deadpanned.

"An' shut down the café," Dud said. "You want some coffee?" Dud got up, disappeared into the kitchen, and returned with two steaming mugs. "They make a decent cup here at the hotel," Dud said. "Not as good as my wife used to make, but here, try it." He handed a cup to Stryker.

"She dead." Stryker asked, returning to asking questions as is his usual laconic, often confusing, if not outright frustrating habit.

"No, she's alive. I came west from Illinois to hunt silver in Virginia City, and she left me. I guess being gone two years was enough for her. She declared abandonment, got a divorce, and married herself a plumber. That was thirty-seven years ago. Haven't had a good cup since." Dud gestured with his mug. "How about you, mister. You married?"

"No." Stryker let it go at that.

They sipped the hot brew in silence, each man perhaps consumed with his own memories. Stryker was, and he figured Dud was, too.

"Thanks for the cup." Stryker sat the empty mug on the little table and rose to his feet. "Reckon I'll ask around, maybe head over to the incline, or Tahoe City. Ferry the best way to get to the incline?" He felt a modicum of kinship with the old man and extended him the courtesy of asking a question with an interrogative.

Stryker left the Whitney House frustrated. All the other jobs he performed for Hearst, he at least knew who he'd have to deal with, or kill. Not this time. He was at a loss where to start. But dammit, someone knew the person, or persons, who put Tami out of business, and it wasn't just the liquor business either. The café posed another piece of the puzzle. Not only did he not know who it was, he had no clue why. He would have to draw them out some way, show themselves, and that would be risky. Risky, because he'd have to be the target. Tami couldn't be one, she might get killed. Yeah, he'd have to be the target.

He figured the best way, in fact the only way for now, would be to go about town asking questions. Put himself out there, highly visible, making him a possible problem, maybe a big problem, for whoever he wanted to find.

[illegible]

[illegible] [illegible] [illegible] [illegible]

[illegible] [illegible] [illegible] [illegible] [illegible]
[illegible] [illegible] [illegible] [illegible] [illegible]
[illegible] [illegible] [illegible] [illegible] [illegible]
[illegible] [illegible] [illegible] [illegible] [illegible]
[illegible] [illegible] [illegible] [illegible] [illegible]
[illegible] [illegible] [illegible] [illegible] [illegible]

[illegible] [illegible] [illegible] [illegible]
[illegible] [illegible] [illegible] [illegible] [illegible]
[illegible] [illegible] [illegible] [illegible]

CHAPTER EIGHT

"What do you know about the tavern fires?" Stryker asked the bartender, as he stood at the bar sipping a beer. The saloon, "The Classy Lassy" on commercial row (Donner Pass Road) was the busiest in town. That's what Dud told him, anyway. A man could get drunk, play poker, or consort with soiled doves there, he'd said to Stryker. If he got desperate enough, Stryker figured, he'd consort with a soiled dove. Part of the job. The saloon was twice as deep as it was wide and had eight or ten tables. Stryker didn't count them. A stove, the newer square kind, sat along the wall opposite the bar on the right side. A few pieces of firewood lay by the stove, but there was no fire. A heavy layer of cigar and cigarette smoke probably warmed the saloon enough to make firing up the stove on a summer night wasn't worth the trouble. Besides, there were plenty of men downing whiskey versions of anti-freeze to keep their bodies warm. At the rear of the saloon was a red door with "Privy" painted in black letters. Multiple wagon wheel lanterns overhead provided light for the card players. There was a piano next to the stove, but no one was playing it. Maybe the night was too young, or the piano player hadn't gotten drunk enough.

"Real tragedies," the barkeep replied. The stout man in his forties wore a white apron, green armbands, and one of those fancy western shirts with lots of rose flowers sewn on it and pearl snap buttons. The smile was genuine enough, though. Polishing a beer glass with a linen cloth, he allowed, "Heard about 'em. Don't know how they started. If you ask me, I think somebody's out to get that woman. Feel sorry for tha' girl." The bartender stopped his polishing and asked, "Why you askin', mister?"

"Curious. I talked with the woman. She seems all right." Stryker slowly rotated the beer glass, then took another sip.

"You did, huh?" The bartender cocked his head, displaying what appeared to be a combination of curiosity and suspicion. He sat the glass under the bar and brought out another to polish. "And she didn't know who was..."

"No," Stryker cut in.

"Pretty strange, pretty damn strange." The barkeep turned from Stryker and stepped along the bar to refill a logger's whiskey glass. He filled two more glasses and returned a few minutes later. "Listen, mister,' he whispered. "Go see Rhonda on Jibboom Street, behind us." He nodded toward the rear door. "Tell her Rono sent you. She works in the second jerker house, a two-story, emerald-green one and gets lots of men with liquor-loosened tongues. Maybe she's heard something. You might give her a few dollars, even if you don't sample her wares." Rono whispered fast and low. He then winked and walked down the bar with an opened whiskey bottle for more pouring.

Stryker drained the last of the beer, sat the glass on the bar top. He turned and leaned against the counter and surveyed the room, searching for suspicious eyes on him. Six tables were occupied with card players who appeared focused on their games. Two more tables had a couple of men at each, and they were being propositioned by "Jezebels" offering their charms. The men looked interested, and did not pay any attention to anyone, or anything, other than the prostitutes. Stryker wondered what the going price was. No one seemed to be interested in him, even though he'd talked loud enough for some to hear. Too bad they might have been someone he could have beaten the shit out of to get information. That is, if he could beat the shit out of someone as weak as he was. He stayed in the saloon a while longer and sat at a table, sipping more beer. When another man came in and sat at the table, Stryker made conversation with him, asking about Tami's fires. He planted seeds.

Mid-afternoon now, and Stryker elected to leave the saloon and pay the girls a visit. He'd gotten no useful information after spending three-and-a-half hours at the table nursing two beers.

He walked from the Classy Lassy onto Donner Pass Road and turned toward Spring Street. He'd guessed right. A few yards up spring, he came to Jibboom. Then, there on his left, second house down, was the two-story greenhouse. The jerky houses looked no different from other houses, with one exception. Each had a red lantern hanging in front. Stryker momentarily wondered why they were called jerky houses. Must be because the soiled doves worked within, plying their *handywork*. No grin fought its way onto the killer's face. He stopped in front of the greenhouse. It had a red door. No sign advertised the pleasures to be had inside. Word of mouth did that.

He climbed the three steps to the front door and knocked. No need to go around back. He wasn't hiding from a preacher or a wife. A comely winch swung the door open. Blond hair hanging straight to her shoulders framed a face that was a little too round. Dressed in a corset, the full-bodied girl in her midtwenties smiled, and with a wide sweep of her arm, invited Stryker to enter.

"You're Rhonda," Stryker said after shutting the door behind him.

The smile fell from the girl's face. "You want Rhonda? I'll go tell her. Wait here." The girl spun and left through two glass doors, beyond which Stryker could see led to a hallway. There were more doors on both sides of the hall, and at the end a banister staircase, angling back toward him, led up to the next floor.

Stryker glanced away from the glass doors and saw five more similarly dressed women resting alluringly in wingback chairs. Four men clumped together in the middle of the parlor gawked awkwardly at the prostitutes. Stryker guessed the men to be loggers by the way they dressed in thick canvas jeans, wool shirts, and suspenders. Instead of western boots made for horse stirrups or for squashing cockroaches in corners, the men wore heavy, round-toed leather boots with deep-soled lugs. They were drunk, and they stunk. A man would want to be first in line in a whorehouse, Stryker reasoned. Decisions and choices were being made by both parties–male buyers and female sellers. The twenty-by-twenty room painted dog-dick red stood bare except for eight emerald-green wingback chairs casually placed around the room. He was idly surveying selections for perhaps another time when Rhonda came through the glass doors.

"You wanted to see me?" She asked. It was clear she was all business and would brook no funny business. "I no longer offer services."

The prostitute who'd opened the front door returned to the parlor and sat in an empty wingback.

Rhonda was at least ten to fifteen years older than the other girls in the parlor. Thinner, she wore a face that had seen its share of hardship during the additional years. She also wore a floor-length dress. She didn't have to say she wasn't for hire; you could easily tell. Just as well, too. Stryker judged this woman would provide sexual favors with an ice pick. Not literally, of course, but it felt like it when they were finished with you. He'd known the type and usually stayed away from them.

"Rono sent me," Stryker stated flatly. His fearsome features, bereft of emotion, gave no hint of purpose when he added, "let's go someplace more private."

Rhonda glimpsed at the other women for any sign of warning and got none. "All right, follow me."

She led Stryker through the glass doors, which had remained ajar, and opened the first door on the left. Inside the room was a desk with books and papers scattered on it. Behind the desk was a wooden swivel chair on rollers. It had slightly concave arms and purple cushions on the seat and back, suggesting Rhonda spent a lot of time in the chair. A single straight-back chair was in front of the desk. A window on the left wall had white-laced curtains held back by laced straps. The window sash was fully raised for airflow and the curtains fluttered in the breeze. Behind the desk chair were two over-sized mahogany bookshelves filled with law books and sundry literary classics. Except for the bookshelves and a stone fireplace by the window, the walls were bare. All four sides of the room were painted forest green. Rhonda slipped around the desk and sat. She rocked back in the chair and rested her hands on the armrests.

No mental lightweight, this Rhonda. Stryker took a seat in the straight-back chair, already feeling disadvantaged.

"What do you want?" Rhonda abruptly asked.

"Who's torching Tahoe Tami's saloons?"

"Why do you want to know?"

"I'll stop 'em." *No sense fuckin' around.*

"I don't know for sure." Rhonda sat forward and put her elbows on the desktop. She clasped her hands together, took a deep breath, and exhaled. "Hmmm. I could be of some help, though."

Shit, she wants to make a deal. "What's the cost?" Stryker didn't hide his annoyance.

Rhonda nodded pensively. "No money, mister. What's your name?"

"Stryker"

"You do a job for me first, Stryker." Rhonda waited for a reply. Stryker remained impassive. She continued. "I had two of my girls run off last night. I want to know where they are, and I want them back."

"You run 'em off?"

"No."

"Why you want them back?" Stryker was curious.

"They're twins, half breeds. Half Paiute, half white. I bought them from a man. Cost me a lot of money to free 'em. The two of them agreed to pay me back by working it off."

"How much?"

"Thousand a piece."

"They must be..."

"Beautiful! Rhonda snapped. Yes, they are."

"You expect me to find them?" Stryker growled.

"Last I heard, they were headed west. Toward California, I guess."

"Train, horse, or wagon."

"Both ridin' one horse. Stole it. And one more thing. They took a silver chalice. It's mine, and it was given to me by the Duke of Bedford. Herbrand, you might know him." Rhonda could be sarcastic.

"He gave it to you." Stryker drawled. He had doubts.

"All right, fat bastard was drunk on ale, and he left it in the room after we... spent the night together. I grew up in Scotland and I was fifteen then. Anyway, it's mine, God-dammit!

"What you tell me when I bring 'em back better be good. Otherwise, I'll..."

"Rhonda!"

The harlot's cry came from the parlor.

"Damn." Rhonda rose from her chair and was rounding the desk when one of the girls rushed into the room.

Stryker quickly got to his feet. He draped his hand over the Colt.

"Gladys! What the hell is it?" Rhonda barked curtly.

"Boone's back." Gladys announced, almost crashing into her boss. "That son-of-bitch is back here again. And of course, he's drunk!"

"That's all we need," Rhonda groused. "He's a mammoth of a man, Stryker. Taller than you. He's a logger, strong enough to man-handle a log that'd take three men to move, I hear. Not a young man now, but he still had lots of muscle with a full scraggly black beard over pockmarked puffy cheeks. He's a fearsome beast." Rhonda opened a drawer and pulled out a handgun. "The bastard also has a nasty habit of laying his full weight on a girl and gripping her throat with one of his meaty hands when he fucks her. Two of my girls have almost died from his lovemaking. One of the girls had permanent damage due to cracked vertebrae. She wore a neck brace. The men seldom chose her. They were afraid they might hurt her. Poor girl had no other way to support herself so she submerged her face in the Truckee River until she drowned." She paused in front of Stryker. "You may have to kill him." Rhonda brushed past Gladys and through the glass doors into the parlor. Stryker followed. Gladys let them both go ahead of her, and then she followed too.

The four prostitutes and their horny loggers quickly filed from the parlor into the hall. The girls led each man to their assigned "work" rooms. They took their men's hands, pulled them inside, and shut the doors behind them. Once inside, the soiled doves went about earning their pay.

That left two prostitutes in the parlor besides Rhonda. So only Boone remained to choose a girl to quell the urgency in his loins. The two slightly smudged doves sat in the wingbacks, heads bowed toward the floor, most likely praying for the other girl to be chosen.

"Boone, get out!" Rhonda yelled sharply.

"Where's Jolene?" Boone yelled in booming, slurred speech.

"She's dead," Rhonda screamed back at him.

"She ain't dead." Boone ran his eyes around the parlor room, apparently searching for the dead girl.

"She is dead, and you killed her!"

Stryker watched impassively, wondering how many .44 slugs it would take to kill the huge man. No way he could take Boone with blades or fists. He was still too weak.

"What you mean I killed her? I ain't killed nobody! Jolene ain't dead, dammit!"

Stryker drifted his forefinger inside the trigger guard and adjusted the Peacemaker for a quick pull.

"Dig up her grave and see for yourself, Boone. You broke her neck, and she killed herself," Rhonda said, lowering her voice.

Boone looked at the other girls, and for the first time saw the tall man standing by the glass doors wearing a Colt on his hip. Neither of the two women nor Stryker hinted that Rhonda had told him anything but the truth. "Jolene? She really dead?" Boone asked, more quietly now. Rage was slinking from his face.

"Cemetery is east of town, beyond the livery, on the hill. It's a new grave, got her name, 'Jolene Sichler' on the tombstone."

"Jolene?" Boone's mouth curled down at the ends. He furrowed his brows and tears welled up in his eyes. He wiped his nose on his sleeve. "I don't want nobody but her." Boone turned and walked out of the whorehouse.

"I actually felt kinda sorry for him," the prostitute, with lots of blond curls, said.

"Well, he damn near killed me too," groused the other harlot, a freckled-face girl in her early twenties. "Fucked me before he fucked Jolene. Now, I'm glad he took a liking to her." When everyone turned to look her way, she added, "I guess I really didn't mean that."

They found Boone's body a half mile down the Truckee River the following week. The swollen body had no wounds which suggested he drown. Jolene's grave had been dug up and the wooden casket opened four days before they found Boone's body. Only Stryker and the working girls in the green jerky house on Jibboom Street connected Boone's death with the grave desecration.

Stryker left Rhonda and her girls, got the roan, and went to Reece's Supply Store. There, he picked up a few provisions. He'd put them in a burlap sack and was hanging it on his saddle horn when Dud walked up.

"Looks like you're headed somewhere, Mister Stryker." Dud said, nodding at the sack. "Got your grub in there?"

Stryker finished tying on the sack and said, "The bartender at Classy Lassy told me to talk to Rhonda at..."

"I know who she is," Dud said with a knowing smile. "What'd she tell you?"

"Nothing, but she knows something," Stryker growled. "Said she'd tell me if I'd bring back a couple of runaway whores."

"Two of 'em 'eh? I saw two black-haired girls riding out of town last night." Dud said. "They was ridin' bareback on an old nag, a Paint I reckon. Might'ta been them. They ain't gonna get far on that horse."

"Heading west?"

"Yep, headin' west."

Stryker bent to adjust a stirrup.

"Good luck to ya," Dud said. "Hope you..." He didn't finish when he saw Stryker wasn't paying him any mind.

Stryker mounted the roan, reined about without a word to Dud, and started out riding west on Donner Pass Road. A quick study of the sun drifting toward the western mountains told him he had about four hours of daylight left. The road loosely paralleled rail tracks, and a train passed by as soon as he got out of town. The big locomotive had already reduced speed from twenty-five miles an hour to around five and was coasting into town. The engine blew puffs of steam out its sides, giving the hulking monster a white mustache. Four coach cars were behind the engine and the tender car. Stryker could see people in the windows looking like puppet heads in a carnival show staring at him. Men and women, mostly men, watched him with casual but curious interest.

An hour after the train lumbered past Stryker, he came to the Eastern edge of Donner Lake. The lake, at two-and-three-quarters miles long and three-fifths of a mile wide, was much smaller than its neighbor, Lake Tahoe, twenty miles away. Looking across the water to the west, Stryker saw the cut along the side of the mountain with train tracks winding down the Sierras from Donner pass. A train trailing black smoke from its engine snaked along the rocky escarpment. It would eventually pass south of the lake on its way to Truckee. At that distance, Stryker thought the train looked like one of those Marklin toy trains he'd seen displayed in New York City's Fifth Avenue Hotel.

He refocused his attention on the road between the roan's ears and tried to estimate how far the half-breed prostitutes could have ridden in one day. Enormously frustrated, that's how Stryker felt. Hearst's lost lover job didn't sit well with him, and now he's off on what could be a wild goose chase. *If that damn woman, Rhonda, got him out of her whorehouse or out of town with a made-up story, he'd kill her.* Although the girls might be slight of build, two on an old horse couldn't travel all that fast, and up ahead at the lake's west end, the road ran to grade and that would slow them even more. The road steepened around twenty miles west of Truckee. That's where they might have to stop after the first day. Moreover, he figured the girls had little or no money. That's why they took the chalice and most likely wouldn't be spending the night at one of the resting stops along Donner Pass Road. Stryker decided to give it a day and a half before he went back to shoot Rhonda.

Light was fading. The sun dropped behind the western mountains a half hour ago, and Stryker had been on the trail for three-and-a-half hours now. With a stop to let the roan rest and have water, he figured he'd ridden about twelve miles. He debated on whether to keep going in the dark or stop for the night. The ride was telling on him. He pushed on, not looking forward to spending a chilly night sleeping on the ground. He might come upon a waystation where he could catch a few winks. Even though they were abandoned when the railroad came through, a few of them remained, and the sturdy log structures would provide shelter. As the road began to steepen, the wind picked up. He tightened his collar and cursed. He cursed the wind. He cursed Rhonda. He cursed the log that injured him. He even cursed Hearst for sending him on such a vain deputation.

Did the roan curse *him* for making it climb Donner Pass Road? The horse had no dog in this fight, Stryker mused to himself. It has a man on its back who wouldn't even give it a name, who now makes it do his bidding. A twitch at the corner of Stryker's mouth couldn't quite form into a grin. The roan began to bob its head, working harder now, as the grade steepened.

Gradually, a cacophony of night sounds began to come to life in the dark. Frogs by the stream that ran next to the road warbled love songs to potential mates. Crickets rubbed their spinney legs together, offering an extraordinarily loud performance with their little instruments. A female fox off in the distance wailed what sounded like a woman's scream. A bird, an owl, or some other raptor took flight as Stryker neared its perch on a tree limb. Stryker couldn't see the bird, but he heard it flapping broad wings on a trip to another, presumably safer roost. A large animal, probably a deer, broke into a run, trampling through the brush ahead of him. Animals were getting away from the approaching man on a horse. Coyotes behind him joined together in a chorus of short, painful-like yelps. The roan got skittish, and Stryker stroked its neck with a reassuring pat. "Easy now." Maybe it picked up the scent of a cougar or one of the many bears roaming about. He urged the big horse forward with a gentle nudge of his heels.

Ahead and higher up the grade, Stryker saw a light, a glow from a campfire or a lantern. Then it vanished. Either it flickered off or it disappeared behind the trees as he rode along. Hard to tell if it was on Donner Pass Road, but he knew the trail made several switchbacks as it wound its way up the mountain. A few minutes later, the light came into view again, closer this time, but not a direct line of sight, more like a reflecting glow of a fire or a lantern. It was still high above him. Clouds drifted across the moon, making it even more difficult to see if the road would eventually lead to the light. It faded from view again.

The wind blew stronger, and it grew colder. Stryker's usual sixth sense, his unique ability to be aware of danger when not fully awake, was failing him. He shook himself to re-ignite his acuity. Once again, that feeling of physical failure haunted him, frustrated him. It hung like a wet blanket wrapped around his shoulders. All other injuries in his past had a reachable, definite recovery, and he had a clear mind as he healed. This time, he had doubts of whether the long period of unconsciousness caused permanent brain damage. Had his mind and body weakened to the point of failure if called upon? He shuddered again.

The next time he saw the firelight, or whatever it was, happened a half hour later. However, now he could make out the rectangular frame of a window bordering the yellow glow. That meant a cabin or way station. And he was reasonably sure the trail would take him to it. Regardless, the roan needed resting, and he'd have to pull up there for a while. The road began a series of lazy switchbacks as it grew steeper. He lost sight of the light again, hidden above the wooded cliff above him. He could no longer spot it like before when he was farther down the mountain, yet he figured the cabin must be directly above him. He finally rounded a curve and spied the cabin and the lit window a quarter mile in the distance. It rested on a plateau with no trees to obscure its view. As Stryker rode nearer, he saw it was a one room structure.

He pulled up the roan in front of a dilapidated log building with a low-slung roof. Even in the pale light, he saw the cabin was in desperate need of repair. If ever used as a paid-for rest stop, it had been years ago. He dismounted and as his boots hit the ground; he realized how much his bones ached. A whinny from another horse came from behind the cabin, and Stryker led the roan around back. A rushing stream flowed not far away and there was a patch of grass nearby. A paint, an old one, with a deeply swayed back, was haltered to one of the posts of a deer skin rack. The rack stood nestled inside a crude three-sided lean-to constructed out of bare tree limbs. Someone had pitched straw on the ground under the shelter, but that appeared to be a long time ago, and there was only a thin layer of it now. Much of the straw was black with rot, still there was probably enough for two horses for one night, and the shed provided a modicum of shelter. He tied the roan to the second post. Unusual for him, for he would normally tend to the horse first, giving it food and water at least, but tonight he would come out and take care of the animal after dealing with whoever was inside the cabin.

He crept around to the front. The door hung at an angle on one hinge. Light from inside escaped through the cracked opening, narrow at eye level and wider by the floor. Stryker pulled the Pacemaker and eased back the hammer. He used his free hand to press on the door, trying to keep a rusty hinge from announcing him. At first, the small room looked empty, then he pushed more on the door, opening it wider. The stone fireplace at the far end of the small cabin had a dying fire, no flames. Only hot coals remained to produce the feint glow in the room.

Stryker scanned inside the cabin. Rough-hewn planking covered the floor and there was only the one window, that being the one emitting firelight Stryker saw from the road. It had no glass. It was just a rectangular opening now. The place was totally bare except for two bodies, diminutive bodies, too small to be men, facing away from him, lying in front of the fireplace. And they wore dresses. He shoved the door wider and slammed it against the wall. The girls stirred a little, adjusted themselves, and then settled back into deep slumbers. No packs, no blankets, no coats. They sure left Rhonda's in a hurry. It appeared they'd been desperate to get away. Certainly, not a lot of planning had gone into the escape. He holstered the Peacemaker and went out to tend to the roan. A few minutes later, he brought in the burlap sack containing provisions he bought in Truckee—coffee, beans, potatoes, cured bacon, hardtack biscuits, and cooking utensils. The girls hadn't moved. He carried the sack to the fireplace and set it by the fire. He looked around, saw no more wood for the fire, and went back out for more. When he returned with an armload of firewood, one girl was awake and staring at the sack he'd placed by the fireplace. She was still staring at it when he dumped the wood on the hearth. Startled, she scooted away from Stryker, though she said nothing.

He went outside to the horses and unsaddled the roan. The paint had no saddle, or any other gear he could find hanging in the shelter, only the halter tied to the lean-to pole. He untied his bedroll wrapped in a canvas tarp and slipped off the saddlebags. Leaving the saddlebags on the ground, he carried the saddle into the cabin.

"You won't make it to California, if that's where you're headed," Stryker drawled. He dumped the saddle a few feet away from the fireplace and picked up a couple of pieces of wood to put on the fire. After a quick glance at the girls, he leaned down to blow on the coals. Flames flickered and burst into life, and he sat back, kneeling on one knee. Resting a forearm on the raised knee, he said, "I want your help and you're gonna give it." Stryker faced toward one of the most striking females he had ever seen. Light from the fire danced in the girl's eyes, eyes the color of the aquamarine water of Lake Tahoe. With hair as black as coal and her high cheekbones, the girl could sure weaken a man's knees.

"Who… Teva?" The second girl stirred.

"A man here, Avet." Teva warned. She looked frightened now.

Avet, at first, propped herself up on an elbow, then she sat up. She brushed a few strands of hair from her face and stared at the kneeling man–a fearsome, unfriendly looking man.

Two of the most striking women he'd ever seen. Stryker poked the coals with another tree branch and added it to the fire. "Not sure that horse you stole will make back to town."

Teva and Avet exchanged glances. They shifted to cross-legged positions and didn't speak. The mixed breed probably didn't come across as the fatherly type.

They looked out of place in dresses. Stryker thought they should be wearing Indian deerskin outfits, colorful and beaded, and the feathered head bands of tribal princesses. That would have been more fitting. "How old are you two?"

"T-twenty," Teva stuttered in reply.

"You have folks?"

"Our parents are dead," Teva said. She didn't offer to explain how they died.

This was not what Stryker expected. These girls, not Rhonda, were the victims. And the so-called valued horse was one step away from glue or dog food–if asked, the owner might have been happy to have the poor beast taken off his hands.

"You hungry?" There was no answer. Stryker knew they must be. He saw no signs of food. "We'll eat and talk later." He left and came back in with the rest of his gear and emptied the contents of the saddlebag on the floor. Stryker picked up a small pot with a wire handle and held it out to Teva. "Wait," he ordered. "Take this too," he said, giving her a camp coffee pot. "Go get water from the stream."

Teva took the pots, got to her feet, and left the cabin to fetch the water.

"What are you going to do with us?" Avet asked. She straightened her dress out over her knees.

"Depends on how willing you'll do what I want. How did you start the fire?"

"We brought matches." Avet added nothing else after that. She just sat quietly and watched Stryker handle the food until Teva came through the door, and then she stared at her sister, walking across the floorboards with the water pots. Avet gave Teva a stilted smile and arched eyebrows as if conveying the eager intensity of someone who wants to report important news or tell a secret.

Teva handed the pots to Stryker. He hung the cooking pot on the iron swivel crane by the fireplace. The cooking crane was about the only accoutrement in the cabin that remain usable. He added a potato in the pot to boil. Grabbing a handful of ground coffee out of a pouch, he dumped the grinds into the coffee pot boiler. Stryker positioned two branches together in the glowing coals and set the coffee pot on them. He pulled a six-inch fry skillet from the saddlebags and laid out three strips of bacon in it. Then he positioned the skillet next to the coffee pot. Stryker left the cabin again and returned with a tarp, saddle blanket, and bedroll. He tossed them on the floor and went back to tending dinner. In a few minutes, the tantalizing aroma of frying bacon and coffee brewing wafted about the room. The potato took longer than the bacon to cook, and Stryker realized he should have boiled it earlier. He set the bacon aside and let the potato boil several minutes more before swinging the cook arm from the fire. The potato wasn't quite done, but he cut it into three pieces, anyway. Stryker never did put much time or effort into preparing a meal. He put the girl's portions on the only tin plate he carried on the roan and ate from the skillet. The coffee cup was passed between all three of them, and Stryker couldn't help but feel a particular intimacy with the shared cup. They got the fork and knife as well, and he noticed the girls struggled mightily not to wolf their meager portions of food.

"You're coming back to Truckee with me," Stryker said when they'd finished eating. "And where's the chalice?"

Avet withdrew a stemmed silver cup from under her dress and handed it to Stryker. Underneath a napkin stuffed in the bottom, he found a bundle of matches. He figured the cup, matches, and horse was the extent of the girl's escape plan. They probably planned to sell the cup for cash at some point.

"Mister..." Teva began.

"Stryker, name's Stryker."

"Mister Stryker." Teva cleared her throat. "We don't want to go back." She sounded resolute.

"You can ride tied up," Stryker drawled.

"We're not prostitutes." Avet tried being assertive as well.

"You're working for Rhonda," Stryker said.

"She bought us from a man. Said we could work for her and pay her back. We didn't know we had to provide sex for men," Teva said.

"The man she bought you from? He owned you?"

"He took us in after our folks got sick and died," Teva replied. "He had us to do chores and other jobs to pay for our upkeep. That was four years ago, when Mister McIntosh got us and took us to his farm in Overton, Missouri to cook and clean house. His wife had died with the cholera too."

"We worked all day, at first just around his house, cooking and cleaning just like he said we'd have to do. Then when we wouldn't do what he told us his wife did for him in the bedroom, he started having us doing farm work, milking cows, feeding pigs and chickens, digging post holes for fences, gathering hay, picking corn, and whatever else he wanted to us to do. We thought it was a punishment for not providing him with sex. But then he started forcing himself on us. We couldn't leave because he always kept one of us chained while the other did work or had sex with him."

Then one day Rhonda came to town. She somehow found out about my sister and me and wanted us to come live with her. She said we could help her in the business she ran in Truckee," Avet chimed in. "We didn't know what kind of business or where Truckee was, but we thought it couldn't be worse than Missouri."

"We were wrong," Teva moaned. "But Rhonda said we owed her two-thousand dollars and if we didn't offer ourselves to the men, we'd go to jail. We ran off after two weeks. That was last night."

"Get some sleep," Stryker said. "I'll decide what to do with you in the morning. You take the tarp and blanket," he said, tossing both to Teva. He took the saddle blanket and laid it out on the floor in front of the fire. After unbuckling his gun belt and pulling off his boots, he stretched out on the blanket with his feet toward the fire. He put the Peacemaker down at the waist of his pants, draped his coat over him, and lay on his side and facing the girls. "Don't run off. Only one of you will survive." About a year ago, Stryker had seen a Cheyenne squaw shoot herself after he'd killed her brave. These half breeds might do the same, if motivated. Here tonight, he thought, leaving one girl alive to grieve would be more of a deterrent than if they thought both would be killed. Grief can be a weighty burden for the survivor. Stryker knew about that.

The girls lay on the tarp and covered themselves with the blanket, feet facing the fire's warmth, but not right next to him. Outside, a wind was coming up and whooshed through the pine trees. Wind blowing through the pines always made a ghostly whir. A gust swooped down the chimney and sent up a shower of sparks from the fire. Lightning flashed somewhere in the distance and a rumble of distant thunder followed three seconds later. Maybe a storm was brewing. Stryker was bone tired. So now he ignored potential ill weather and listened to the fire crackle and pop, sending embers up the chimney. Firelight figures danced on the wall behind the girls. He knew the girls couldn't yet be asleep, and he wondered if they were scheming for an escape during the night. His last thought before his eyelids closed for the night was whether he or the girl's horse outside was more exhausted.

Thunder rolled closer, sounding more and more like artillery fire. In his dream, the rumbling morphed into cannon fire. Up and down the line, on Cemetery Ridge, Union forces were deployed in the J-hook formation. At fifteen, a young Stryker commanded the gun crew of a ten-pound Parrott rifle. His gunnery sergeant and the two corporals had been killed in the cornfield at Antietam. Now Stryker gave orders to three other men, boys actually, not much older than he. The Confederates advanced across a mile of open ground. On they came, in their hot wool uniforms, running and yelling their Rebel Yell in a single column formation. Pickett's Charge it was famously called. Dumbass Charge, Stryker remembered that day. With the North's heavy fire directed at the front of the column, the Rebel line staggered forward. Men in the rear ranks advanced, stepping over a growing pile of dead, and the column simply erased itself as it moved across the open field. Heavy rifle and cannon fire shrouded the ridge in smoke, and from the smoke, bullets and shrapnel shot out to tear into thousands of gray uniforms. Hot steel and blood. Finally, the Rebel attackers broke and ran, leaving 60 percent of the column lying on the field. The poor bastards.

"Fire!" Stryker yelled the command every twenty seconds and the Parrott Rifle belched beehives of steel. He tried to shout the orders with a command voice, but his young vocal cords failed him and his firing orders came out as screeches. A couple of the crew giggled at his high-pitched voice until a bullet ripped through one of the boy's Adam's apple, then he fell to the ground and choked to death on his own blood. Thunder kept roaring. Cannons kept firing. Men kept dying.

Finally, the storm outside moved up the mountain and his dreamed battle grew quiet.

That's when a delicate caress on his cheek and a soft breath on his forehead woke Stryker. Another hand brushed the hair from his face. Fingertips moved gently about his groin. *Another girl's hand? Am I really awake?* Stryker slid his hand to the butt of the Colt.

"Just lie there and enjoy," Avet whispered in his ear.

Now this is where some men, a few prudish, self-righteous men, might say, "Get away from me you naughty girls. I'm not that kind of man." Those are not the kind of men you would want to have a drink with. What the hell would the two men talk about? And if the truth be known, most women (*maybe all!*) wouldn't want a man like that either. Most women want a man who will scratch her itch.

Well, Stryker is no prude. *She told me "Lie" instead of "Lay." Good grammar. Proper. I must act properly as well and do what she says.* Stryker used inscrutable logic here.

Avet leaned closer and planted light kisses on Stryker's forehead. Her hands continued their angelic caresses about his face. Teva's fingers toyed with the buttons on his fly. Stryker withdrew the Peacemaker from his pants and laid it beside him. He did keep his hand resting on it.

Teva undid his belt buckle. Then she let her fingers trace his growing erection outside the denim. Knowledgeable tease, Stryker mused. Fast learners, these girls. No wonder Rhonda wanted them back. Teva walked her fingers to the top button. It took a little effort, and she struggled with it until it popped free. She worked her way down the rest of the buttons. In the meantime, Avet planted light kisses on his face to where her lips found his. Her velvety lips floated onto his and parted, allowing her tongue to roam lightly inside his mouth. By now, Teva freed his penis from the shortened long johns. Stryker wore a pair with the legs cut off above the knees and arms trimmed above the elbows in the summer. The cool air exacerbated the erotic sensation coming from his exposed manhood. She gingerly wrapped her hand around it beneath the head and slowly stroked. *You naughty girls.* The sensual pleasure, simultaneously administered by the twins, was electrifying. Shock waves radiated from the small of his back, tingling his testicles and making his penis jerk with excitement. Rock hard. He had to struggle mightily against premature ejaculation. Teva lowered her mouth to the head of his cock while she continued to stroke him, and it didn't take long for his resolve to fail. It *had* been quite a while since he'd drained things. A moment later, Teva spit in the fire. No tissue, and Teva surely didn't want to soil her dress. So, the girl made a practical decision.

When they tried to do more, he stopped them. "You've done enough. I'll arrange it so you don't have to work for Rhonda." He reached that conclusion not for what they just did, but for the sacrifices they'd made. He wasn't cocky enough to figure they enjoyed it. Their desperation touched the callous mixed breed. *I'm one tough son-of-bitch, all right.* He stood up, shaking his head as he buttoned his trousers, and then he went to go check on the horses. He put the Colt in the holster and left the gun belt in the cabin.

Outside, Stryker wanted to be sure the roan and paint hadn't been spooked by the storm. Both horses remained tied to skinning poles, and upon running a hand down their front and rear leg fetlocks, he found nothing suspicious. Once satisfied the horses were okay, he straightened and stroked the roan's muzzle. Was he trying to be a better man or was his thinking just coming from his groan? He returned to the cabin, gathered up the saddle blanket, and went back outside to wipe down the horses. While he was out, Teva and Avet curled back into their blanket. Upon returning, their rhythmic breathing told him girls had fallen asleep. Stryker hung the saddle blanket next to the fireplace to dry and lay down on the rough-hewn floor. He pulled his coat over him and within a few minutes, fell asleep, feeling quite satisfied.

The following morning, the three cabin occupants stirred from sleep at approximately the same time. A cold chill greeted them in the cabin and their breaths came out in small vaper puffs. Wide streams of sunlight had broken through the pine trees, making it warmer outside the cabin than it inside. Stryker slid forward toward the smoldering fire and tried to bring it back to life by blowing on it. No good. He picked up a few twigs from what was left of the branches he'd brought in before. After scuffing the tips on the fireplace rock and he shoved them in the coals. The coal chars looked gray on the surface, but Stryker figured they might still have enough heat within to rekindle the fire. Smoke rose from where he'd buried the twigs and soon a small flame broke through. He shoved more pine logs in the nascent fire and set two of them side by side near the front for cooking breakfast.

"Did you mean what you said last night?" Teva asked, sitting up and sweeping hair from her face. The girl's countenance reflected her anxiety. "You're not taking us back to work for Rhonda?" Avet perked up from under the blanket. She crawled out to sit by her twin, both eager to hear Stryker's answer.

"Told you that. Don't ask me again," Stryker said, still trying to decide whether his cock was doing all the thinking.

"Well, will you take us to California?" Avet asked. She glanced hopefully at Teva.

"No, dammit." However, what Avet asked gave Stryker pause. Details, he'd have to work out the details. The biggest problem had to do with Rhonda. She may not go for what he had in mind. In fact, he knew she wouldn't. He might have to use persuasion. Stryker wasn't in the habit of using force on a woman. Okay, that was a lie. He'd killed a few. He liked to think they deserved it, though.

"We'll eat and head back. Gave you my word. Meant it."

The twins eyed each other and said nothing. Finally, Teva asked, "you want more water for the coffee?"

Stryker picked up the coffee pot from the hearth and shook it. "There's enough to heat." He dumped a handful of coffee grounds into the pot and placed it on the two branches. Flames eagerly licked around the bottom third of the coffee boiler where it had been blackened by a thousand cook fires. He handed his metal cooking pot to Teva. Fill that up with about one-fourth water."

Teva left, returning a few minutes later. She handed Stryker the pot and water. He untied a cloth pouch and emptied two handfuls of gruel into the pot. He set it on the two branches next to the coffee that had boiled. Ten minutes later, Stryker said, "this is breakfast." He wrapped a cloth on the pot handle and pulled the gruel from the fire. Servings in the plate and pot were the same as before, so was the shared coffee cup.

After breakfast, Stryker gave the Teva and Avet the cooking utensils to wash in the stream while he saddled the roan. When they returned, he packed the pots and cutlery and what was left of the provisions into the saddlebags. He helped them onto the bare back of the Paint and handed Teva, who rode in front, the halter, and then he swung onto the roan. He figured both girls were slight enough to not shift the loads. In the bright light of day, Stryker saw their eyes were even more beautiful, and he caught himself staring at them more than once. When his gaze inadvertently lingered, they dipped their heads, obviously embarrassed. That bothered him. He didn't know if it was because of his staring or what they'd done the night before that caused their embarrassment. He finally decided it was probably both, and he stopped staring.

Going downhill was easier for the old paint. It made it to Truckee. The girls led Stryker to where they'd first taken the poor animal and left it there. It was late afternoon now. Although they had not eaten anything since the meager breakfast, he dismounted the roan and walked the twins to the train station. The one-story wooden building painted yellow ran alongside the tracks for roughly forty feet. An elevated platform with a ramp leading onto it from the side extended beyond the building so that livestock and freight could be loaded onto boxcars. Stryker tied off the roan and walked Teva and Avet into the station. The ticket master stood behind a window with brass bars on their right. The clerk didn't bother to look up as they came inside. There were no other windows in the building and on the walls were posters advertising train destinations and times for departures and arrivals. Four long wooden benches ran vertically from the ticket window for travelers to sit and wait for trains. A family of four, five men outfitted in logging clothes, and an elderly man dressed in a black suit reading a bible, were all seated on the benches. The family set on the front bench, at the far end opposite the ticket window, and apart from the loggers and the preacher. Stryker guided the girls to a rear bench behind the family of four.

"Sit here until I return," he ordered. "Don't say shit to anybody. I'll be back in a few minutes." With that, he left.

Teva and Avet watched the mixed breed walk out of the station. "I guess we better stay here," Teva whispered to her sister.

"I'm hungry," Avet whispered back.

"Me too, but let's wait." Teva circled an arm around her sister.

Outside the station, Stryker swung into the saddle and headed to Rhonda's. Down Donner Pass Road, stores and shops were closing doors, merchants calling it a day, and there was piano music blaring out from some of the thirty-something saloons. Wafting out from one of the watering holes was off-key singing of a woman. She warbled a sad love song, a forlorn tune, appropriate for eliciting salty tears into beer glasses. Loggers jumped off wagons they'd ridden into town from a hard day's cutting. Truckee was revving up for another raucous evening. Stryker rode on and swung the roan over to Jibboom Street. He pulled up in front of the two-story greenhouse.

The front door was ajar. Something' not right. Stryker's body tensed. His pale eyes squinted. He eased from the saddle, drew the Peacemaker, and climbed the three steps to the red doors. The door hung six inches open, and he eased it wider with his free hand. A man stood in the middle of the floor, back to him, holding a revolver and pointing it at four soiled doves huddled around a wingback chair. The frightened whores stared at the man between Stryker and the wingback, and none noticed Stryker slip inside. Raised voices of more men came from beyond the glass doors. Angry threats directed at another person.

Stryker holstered the Colt and pulled the razor. The shouting beyond the glass doors covered him, moving up behind the man. Stryker cupped the man under his chin and at the same time, jammed his boot into the back of the man's knee. He fell back against Stryker's chest and before the startled man could yell or fire his gun, the mixed breed slit his throat. The gun thudded to the floor.

The frightened harlots were too shocked to scream, and Stryker brought a forefinger to his lips, signing them to stay that way. The dying man's gurgling wasn't loud enough to send a warning to the other men, and his feeble coughing died out completely as Stryker took three quick strides to the glass doors.

Stryker pushed down on the handle and eased the door open. The door to Rhonda's office stood ajar, but because of the angle, he couldn't see the men making the threats. He stepped into the hall and edged up to the door. Two more working girls peered out from rooms down the hall. Stryker pressed a forefinger to his lips again.

He raised the dripping razor and peeked into the room. Two men. Their backs were turned to him, but he recognized the two men he'd seen earlier in the Classy Lassy, Mikhail and Kirill. Kirill was asking the questions. It sounded as if they were asking about him. Mikhail was doing the persuading. Rhonda sat in the swivel chair with her wrists bound to the chair arms. Her legs were spread and drawn rearward, with her ankles tied to the rear chair legs. The madam's dress was pulled up to her waist and bunched there, exposing her pink stockings and white thighs. Rhonda's face looked lumpy and swollen with purple bruises caused by several blows. Blood seeped from the corner of her mouth, and by the appearance of her mangled mop, it she'd been yanked about by the hair.

"Now, we get to real persuading'," Kirill sneered.

Mikhail jerked Rhonda's head back. "You listen to him?"

Kirill dropped his hand to the hunting knife on his hip and handed it to Mikhail. "Enlarge her twat so she can handle big ones."

Stryker switched the razor to his left hand and drew the Peacemaker. He figured, what the hell, there were lots of shootings in Truckee. Gunfire coming from the house would hardly be noticed.

The .44 slug drilled into the back of Mikhail's head and exited out his left eye. The second slug smacked into Kirill between his shoulder blades. He spun around and Stryker gifted him another bullet in his chest, right of center, and Kirill fell to the floor dead.

Stryker stepped around the two bodies and lifted Rhonda's chin. Her battered face in clear view now showed the full damage she'd suffered. A fireplace poker lay on the desk and there was blood on the tip. "You awake, woman?"

Rhonda tried to speak. With lips swollen twice their normal size, her words came out mushy. She nodded.

"I brought the girls and the chalice. You can have the cup."

Rhonda held up two fingers, then quickly added a third. "Three-thousand dollars," she blubbered. Blood bubbled from her mouth and ran down her chin.

Stryker gripped the poker and raised it over his head. "Reckon they beat you to death before I got here." His eyes narrowed to icy slits. His lips curled back in a cruel grin. He wasn't faking the threat.

At this point, Rhonda made a wise decision. "Stanek. His name's Stanek, and he runs a logging company in Incline." She licked some of the blood from her lips and swallowed it. "Please untie me."

Stryker ignored the request and went out to retrieve the chalice from his saddlebags. When he returned through the glass doors, one of the whores in the hall had advanced to Rhonda's office. She stood by the open door with a towel wrapped around her and was watching her boss bleed.

"Go in," Stryker growled.

Startled, the disheveled prostitute, who'd apparently been interrupted by her work, turned around to face Stryker. "What'll I..."

"Shut up and go in." Stryker looked past her and saw a man peeping from the room she probably came out. The fellow had bare shoulders, and the rest of him was most likely naked too. Coitus interruptus. Stryker swung his gaze back to the curious whore. "Get a wet wash rag to clean her face. Put ice on it." He didn't tell the woman they had ice for chilling the beer in the Classy Lassy. Hell, a man like Stryker can only go so far being helpful.

The harlots in the parlor hadn't moved. They'd sat mortified and watched a man gurgle the last of life's blood from the gaping throat wound. The girls looked up at Stryker when he banged open the glass doors. A pane fell out and shattered on the floor.

"Any you girls know a man called Stanek?" Stryker stepped over the body, being careful not to slip in the blood, and stood in front of the soiled doves.

They shook their heads side to side. The soiled doves sat huddled together looking pretty frightened.

Stryker spun about, stepped over the bloody mess again, and headed out the front door. Once outside the greenhouse of immense pleasure, he set course for the train station. He found Teva and Avet where he'd left them. The two girls were the only people now sitting in the station. Instead of going to speak with them, he went to the ticket window. No one was behind the window, and he clanged the Peacemaker's barrel between the brass bars.

"All right, dammit!" An unseen male groused. From inside a small room to the right, a chair scrapped the floor. Then the ticket master wearing a black cap came out of the room. He had a white napkin stuffed in the top of his shirt. The agent saw the gun barrel pointed at his chest and raised his arms. He continued chewing what he was eating. Must have been good.

Stryker holstered the Colt. "The next train to San Francisco."

The agent, a very thin, balding fellow, dropped his hands and swallowed his food. "In four hours. It's the midnight run."

"Price," Stryker said.

"Seven-fifty."

"Gimme two." Stryker dug into his pocket and counted out fifteen dollars. "I want paper and pencil."

The agent hesitated, but then pulled out a piece of paper and handed it to Stryker. "And here's a pencil," he said, pushing it under the bars.

Stryker took the writing material and sat on a bench. He wrote, *"Find a job and a place to live for these two girls. They're in danger here and they helped me find the arsonist burning Tami's taverns."* Signed, *"Stryker."* He folded the paper in two and wrote *"Senator George Hearst"* on one side of the fold. He rose to his feet and went over to the girls.

"Go to the Palace Hotel in San Francisco." He handed two tickets to the girls. "You're getting on a train headed there in four hours. When you get to the hotel, give this paper to Senator Hearst, personally, if you can. Don't leave the station before you get on the train." He dug into his pocket and withdrew more paper money. "Here's forty dollars for when you get there." Stryker left the twins in the station never saw them again. He never asked about them either.

By now, night fall was settling in on Truckee, and its raucousness was being ratcheted to a much higher level. A drunk man staggered from the Classy Lassy and fell on his knees to retch. Stryker walked on and climbed the steps to the Whitney House. He intended asking the desk clerk for Tami's whereabouts but then saw her eating in the dining room. He strode over to her table and scraped back a chair.

"What do you know about this Stanek man?" Stryker asked, seating himself.

"Stanek?" Tami scrunched her face and cocked her head. "Gosh, I don't believe I know him." She cut into her steak.

"Has a logging company in Incline."

"Incline?" Tami lifted a bite of the steak and held it poised by her mouth.

"Could be a Russian." Stryker waved off a waiter.

"Russian... I think I met a man who could have been Russian. He had an accent that might have been... but why would he do the fires?" Tami asked, biting into the meat.

"He must hate your guts."

"I only saw him the one time," Tami said, swallowing. She laid the fork aside. "It was a year or more ago. He was an ugly, course man. He came into my tavern with some other loggers. They all talked with what I thought were European accents. But I didn't even talk to him."

"Rhonda, she runs a whorehouse. Said he's the man who's been burning you out."

"Never met her. Is she sure?" She wouldn't just say that, would she? I mean, maybe she doesn't like him for some reason."

"She might. Three Russian types were going to beat her to death yesterday. Didn't see a particular ugly one."

Suddenly, Tami looked serious. "Beat her to death?"

"They wanted information, apparently. Don't know if she told 'em or not. If she did, they didn't believe her."

"You said they were going to kill her. They didn't? Why not?"

"I killed *them*."

Tami straightened and stared at the mixed breed. She set the fork down.

"I'll head over to Incline. In the meantime, don't leave the hotel, and don't be alone," Stryker said. "I want the quickest way there and back. Tell me."

"Take the steamer. It leaves Tahoe City for Incline twice a day at eight in the morning and two in the afternoon."

Tami watched as Stryker scooted back his chair and got to his feet. "Why are you helping me? Who are you?"

"Do what I said. I'll be gone a day." Stryker was off saying nothing more, and Tami didn't, or couldn't, think of another question to ask.

Stryker walked from the hotel and swung onto the roan. It was going to be a long night. A fourteen-mile ride and he'd have to rest the roan at least once. He was hungry and tired. Figured the roan was too.

He got to Tahoe City bone tired at three-thirty in the morning. Nothing was open, not even a saloon. There weren't that many of them, two to be exact. Tahoe City hadn't the lively reputation of Truckee. He stopped at a water trough for the roan and then continued to the Gypsy wagon, a little less than two miles farther. Stryker wasn't sure why he needed to see the women, maybe they'd give him food, give him sorely needed strength, maybe he'd let them know he meant what he said about taking them to San Francisco, or maybe he just wanted to see June and her daughter before he boarded the steamer. So, for reasons not really fixed in his head, he reined the roan south to the Gypsy wagon.

The wagon camp lay quiet. There was no lantern light at four in the morning. A clear sky and a full moon silhouetted the wagon against a lunar river in the lake. No doubt the woman and her daughter were asleep, Stryker figured. He slid off the roan and climbed the short steps to the door. It was open.

"June!" Stryker yelled. No need for a gentle greeting. Something is not right here. "June!"

It was pitch black inside the wagon. Even with his eyes already adjusted for night vision, he couldn't clearly make out anything. He yelled a third time, louder. "June!"

There was a moan. A woman's moan. Then, "Stryker?"

"Yes, June."

"Please, Stryker. We need help," June sobbed from the dim interior.

Stryker threw a leg over the bench seat and stepped inside. June had to be hurt. She made no effort to come to him. He tripped over a chair, and then another.

"I'm over here. On the bed," June groaned.

Stryker stumbled over pots and pans strewn on the floor. He felt like cursing out loud, but held back. Stumbling and cursing to himself, he finally made it to the bed and June. His hands touched the mattress. Using one hand to steady himself, he searched for her with the other. He found a thigh. It felt smooth and soft, and naked. He fought the temptation to caress the alluring skin. June shifted her leg, and yelped in pain.

"My ankle might be broken." June took his hand. Not hard. Gentle like, and she guided his hand away from her leg. "Stryker, men came. Three of them. We fought them, but it was no use." June's voice hardened. "And they took Sarah." She kept hold of his hand.

"How long ago?"

"Right at dusk. I can't stand, Stryker. They left me and took her. She was screaming for me. You've got to find her and bring her back." June was talking fast. She tightened her grip.

That meant several hours ago. They've had their fun with the girl and killed her by now, Stryker figured. "June, your daughter may not be alive." He told her that not only because he knew it was probably the truth, but he felt he should stay with June and tend to her injuries. Though she would have to tell him what to do. *The eight o'clock steamer is no good now. Maybe I can make the 2 o'clock boat. Shit. But I have to help this woman with what she did for me.*

"Where's a lantern?"

"On a shelf about halfway down, on the left. Stryker, you've got to go after Sarah now, please!" June cried.

"Which way did they go?"

"South, I think." June pointed, but Stryker couldn't see it in the dark. "I can still hear Sarah screaming as they took her. Stryker, you've got to go now!"

The lantern was still on the shelf with a box of matches near it. Stryker lit the lantern and brought it back to June's bed. When the light hit her, he saw the damage done to June's face. It was grotesquely swollen, and even in the dim light, he saw the red and blue skin. One cheek was split and the cheekbone had burst through the swelling. Her nose looked like a bloody mushroom. A flash of anger tore through him. Over the years of a tragic and brutal past, Stryker's emotions dulled to where few things elicited a reaction. This one did.

"All right. I'll see if I can find her." What he meant was he would find the men and kill them.

Stryker wet a washcloth and applied it to June's battered face. Then he placed pillows under her leg to relieve the pain. He also retrieved a bottle of cocaine medicine June told him get. She took the bottle, poured out two pills, and swallowed them. Stryker guessed she wanted to go with him if she could stand the pain. "You're not going with me."

"Please then, throw something over me and go." June's arms were crossed in front of her breasts. Pain in her leg must have taken precedence over inhibitions. She hadn't quibbled when Stryker positioned her and the pillows. Severe pain trumps modesty.

Stryker chided himself for not covering the woman's nakedness earlier. Her clothing, having been ripped from her, was in shreds. He pulled a sheet over her.

"I'll be fine. Just go." June said. She was trying to act calm now–a doctor's creed.

"I'll be back."

The three men with Sarah hadn't gone far. Eager to assuage lust in their loins, the men stopped not more than a mile down the lake's coastline. Just far enough to isolate daughter from mother so that it was useless for Sarah to keep crying out and spoil the lovemaking. They came to a grassy area and hopped from their horses, whooping and hollering like the crazed drunks they were. They had their fun.

Stryker, over the years, had learned to temper his emotions. Good or bad, he'd kept his reactions to events unaffected by excessive sentiment. Tonight, his resolve would be tested. These women had saved his life. They'd asked for nothing in return. And now he'd brought what was sure to be unfathomable tragedy into their lives. If it hadn't been for him, they would not still be here at the lake. Anger at the men who took Sarah, yes. But anger at himself was even greater.

Stryker heard a horse nicker off to his right and dismounted. He tied off the roan and advanced on foot toward where he figured the nickering horse might be.

The bright moonlight made it easier for Stryker to find three saddled horses grazing in grass. He found the men and the girl's body lying close by. Her dress remained pulled up around her neck and she was naked below that. Sarah was dead, her head bashed in, probably with the melon-sized rock next to her. The men took turns on her until their cocks grew soft and her sobbing became an irritant. So, they killed her and went to sleep.

All three of the men snored loudly, as if in competition with one another.

Stryker pulled the razor. The first man he knelt next to was on his back, snoring the loudest of the three. He was a big man with a full beard. Stryker clapped a hand over his open mouth and dug the tip of the razor into the man's throat. Dragging the blade across the neck in one quick stroke, he sliced through the windpipe. The dying man's eyes flashed open. His meaty hands tore at Stryker's grip on his mouth. He grunted, or at least he tried to grunt an angry curse. The grunt got detoured out of his throat, riding a torrent of blood, and Stryker watched him die before he removed his hand. The man's hands fell away. That was his last movement. His eyes remained open, staring blankly at the stars.

Stryker killed the second killer, also a full-grown man, without even as much as a whimper from him. He never woke up before he died.

The third snorer wasn't a man, but a boy. Stryker stood over him and figured the youth was no more than sixteen. He knelt beside the kid, holding the razor dripping blood on the boy's shirt.

The kid opened his eyes. Saw Stryker above him. Saw the razor. "I didn't do nothun'. I swear. I was jus' with them. I never touched her!"

Stryker knelt and flattened the blade against the boy's neck.

"Please, mister."

Stryker righted the blade, pushed the tip in, and slowly drew it across the kid's throat. Stryker rose and walked away before the boy finished dying.

"Stryker?"

"Sarah?" Stryker ran over and kneeled down beside the girl. "Sarah? I thought you were..."

"They hurt me, Stryker." She released a soft groan and then lay still.

He put his hand on her neck. Then he leaned down and placed an ear on her bare chest. There was nothing. *The last word on her lips was his name. It was too familiar.* He stared at the girl's body for a long minute and then got to his feet.

Stryker walked to the lake water's edge and fell to his knees. He looked up at the sky, at the stars. "Why, God? She was just a girl. An innocent girl, God. Why, Dammit? Damn you! Where's your fucking mercy? What kind of God are you? You let this happen! You made it happen! Why'd you do it? You should have killed me instead with that damn log!" Stryker fell forward to all fours, his body shaking. No tears–tear ducts dried up years ago. Then he started dry retching.

When that ended, he sat back on his heels. He stopped shaking. He'd gotten no answer. Nothing. *I can't bring myself to think you're not real, God. But I'm sure as hell mad at you, dammit.*

He felt drained.

A few minutes later, Stryker lifted Sarah's body and draped it over the roan in front of the saddle. He climbed up behind and started the ride back to June. He left the three men in the grass with their empty balls and their slit throats.

Leaving Sarah's body on the roan, he climbed the steps to the Gypsy wagon with weighted effort. News was not good.

June rose to an elbow when Stryker came inside. The welcoming smile drained away, and her face morphed to dark, clouded anxiety. "Sarah's dead?"

"Yes."

June covered her mouth with a hand and sobbed–but only for a moment. With the greatest of effort, she collected herself, and asked, "did you bring her back?"

"On the roan." Stryker said, as he neared the grieving woman. "I'll wrap her in a blanket and bring her in. I'll hitch up the mules, and we'll bring her into town for a proper burial." Driving to town gave him a chance to make the eight o'clock steamer.

"How did she...?"

"Die? Looks like they hit her head with a rock."

"And those men?" June's voice hardened.

"They're dead."

"How?"

Stryker guessed June wanted them to die badly. "I slit their throats."

"You sure they're...?"

"Razor cut deep. Sliced the jugulars." *She'd know about severed jugulars.*

June showed a brief look of satisfaction, then her face hardened again. "I want to see her."

"No. June, you should remember Sarah the way you've known her, not how she looks now. What is out there now is just a body. Sarah is no longer in it. Maybe after the undertaker does his work. But remember what I told you." He let that sink in and then asked, "You need anything else before I bring up the mules?"

"Some water. I'm thirsty."

She must have put up one hell of a fight. "Where is it?" Stryker turned to look for the water.

"In a bucket on the floor next to the door."

Stryker grabbed a cup off the shelf. The table had been knocked over and what had been on it lay strewn about the floor. For a moment, he thought of having Sarah pick things up while he drove the wagon. *You dumb ass.* He dipped the cup in the bucket and brought the water to June.

Not much else to say, he reasoned, and he went out to retrieve Sarah's body. He lifted the dead girl off the roan first and laid it on the ground. He grabbed the blanket and rope from his saddle, wrapped her body in the blanket, and secured it with the rope. He picked up the blanketed burden, *weighing far more than its ninety-eight pounds*, carried it inside, and placed it on the floor by June's bed.

He'd try not to jostle June and her injured leg during the ride to Tahoe City. The first few hundred yards to town were on an upgrade. He let the mules pull at their own pace and only used the reins to guide the animals around rocks or roots he saw in the moonlight.

Was he being a good man? Stryker had self-recriminations. Helping June was good. Though he wished he could do more for the poor woman. And if he hadn't told her to wait a week for him, her daughter would still be alive. That wasn't good. What good he was doing now could no way make up for that. *Fuck.* Killing those three men, that was good. He couldn't help thinking he should have drunk some of their liquor—if any was left—and pissed it on their faces. That would have been really good. Aw hell, he thought, there wasn't time and besides, he could only do so much good.

At times, Stryker heard June talking. He couldn't discern what she was saying, but he could tell by the conversive tempo of her voice she was carrying on a conversation with her daughter. Mixed in with the words, Stryker heard intermittent cries of anguish. Fresh and raw pain. Grief like that overwhelms a person. Takes over your entire being. Like a sharp knife that stabs the heart, and not just once—it keeps stabbing. Takes away your breath til you choke. Yeah, thought Stryker, it's that kind of pain. He knew. He'd had it when Leigh died. It was still there. Changed him forever. It would change June too. He thought about stopping to comfort the woman. She'd already lost her husband and now her daughter. It wouldn't help, even if he knew what to say or do. It was too new. June would have to wear herself out and fall asleep exhausted. He drove on.

They arrived in Tahoe City before the sun peeked over the mountains. June had settled down, or so Stryker thought. He halted the wagon near a house with two signs on one post. One sign read "Dentistry," the other read "Mortuary." Stryker wondered how the dentist business was holding up. He turned around, retrieved the lantern he'd stored behind the driver's bench, and lit it. That's when he saw June had gotten from the bed and was lying next to her daughter's body. He slid from the bench and went to the grieving mother. June had her arm wrapped around the blanket and had fallen asleep. Stryker is one cold-hearted son-of-bitch to be sure, but...

His angst wasn't just for June. Leigh, beautiful but bloodied and mortally wounded, flashed in his mind. Her eyes had fluttered open. She'd said his name and then died. Jagged-edged grief. It still cut deep, even after all the years. Oddly, he almost welcomed it. It kept Leigh's memory alive, but it was a crushing weight. Stryker eased closer to June and dropped to his knees. *We have something in common, June.* He moved the lantern closer and touched her bare shoulder. Didn't shake her, though, he just rested his hand on her until she woke.

"C'mon, June." Stryker set the lantern aside and gently rolled June away from Sarah's body. She'd slipped from the bed, leaving the sheet strewn behind her, and was partially uncovered. He gathered the sheet around her again, slid his arms underneath, and lifted her back to the bed. "We're in town. Lay there. I'll get help." He moved to the front of the wagon before turning around. "Don't leave the bed again dammit!" Stryker gave and received strict orders in the military, stern commands to demand obedience and overcome fear. Maybe it would work on grief as well.

Night gave way to a gray dawn in Tahoe City. It seemed colder than when it was totally dark, usually does for some reason. A single-story white clapboard building set back from the street and had two wooden caskets leaning against its front wall. Two horses were standing in a corral on the far side of the house and buckboard wagon was parked outside the gate. Stryker assumed that's where dental work and embalming took place. They'd started embalming the dead in the Civil War to ship the bodies home and it became common practice after the war. Stryker guessed the dentistry business was slow and whoever ran the place moonlighted as a mortician. He hopped off the wagon, quick-stepped to the house with the caskets, and knocked on the door. No answer. He went around to the front of the bigger house and banged on its door. Nothing. He waited half a minute and kicked in the door. Stryker held back, going inside, figuring he might meet a loaded gun, and instead yelled through the opening, "Answer the God-damn door!"

"Who's out there? What you want?" A man bleated from a back room.

"Got two women. One hurt, one dead."

"Go help him, Winford," a woman said. She sounded more authoritative than the man.

"Gotta put on some clothes, dammit!" The bedsprings creaked. "How bad is the one hurt?"

"Broken leg." Stryker thought leg sounded more dire than ankle. "She's in a lot of pain."

"Okay, I'm comin'. Putin' on my shoes."

A short, thin man emerged from the bedroom. He couldn't clearly be seen until he got to the door. The dentist-mortician wore a white shirt and black wool pants with suspenders and horned rim glasses. He glanced at the shattered wood surrounding the door lock, and then at Stryker. "Where is she?" Winford asked, looking a bit nervous.

"In the wagon."

"Bring her 'round to the building in back, please." Winford had gotten a good look at Stryker and decided to be more pleasant.

By the time Stryker got June out of the wagon and carried her to the smaller building, the multi-disciplinarian had the door unlocked and a lantern lit. Stryker brought June in and laid her on a long, flat table. June had clenched her teeth together but she couldn't hold back a shrill moan when he stretched out her injured leg. Stryker saw a pile of towels on a wall shelf and grabbed two. He put one under June's leg and the other one under her head.

A metal tank, which looked a lot like a sheep trough, was next to the table. Stryker had seen them used in the war to embalm the dead. A makeshift dentist chair sat facing a side window. Most likely positioned there for better light. By one wall a lit lantern sat on an oak desk where books and sketches of anatomy drawings lay scattered. Three drawers were stacked down its left front, and one deep drawer hung on its other side. Hanging on pegs along the opposite wall were jackets, shirts, pants, ties, and belts for men, and a few dresses for the ladies. They provided extra clothing for dressing up the dead. Nothing too fancy. The dead weren't all that particular.

"Mister, I gotta tell you. I'm not a regular doctor, not even a real dentist. I give 'em a cocaine pill and yank out their teeth," Winford kind of warned.

"Bring the lantern and look at my ankle," June said. She propped herself up on an elbow to watch.

"Okay, but like I tolt you, I don't have formal training. My father was a dentist. I jus' watched him til he died. I was twelve. I…"

"She's a doctor," Stryker growled.

"You are?" The not-quite dentist asked, looking relieved. He brought the lantern from the desk.

"What's your name?" June asked.

"Winford, ma'am."

"Just do what I tell you, Winford."

Because of poor lighting and trauma, June hadn't taken a closer look at her foot. All she knew was it hurt and she couldn't stand on it. Now she sat up and examined it. Her foot lay on the table, twisted at an odd angle. The ankle appeared discolored and deformed. The end of the upper bone stuck on the side. "It's dislocated, Winford."

"Dislocated," Winford repeated, staring at the ankle.

Stryker figured Winford was at a loss what to do.

"You're going to work it back into the socket, Winford," June said.

"Don't you think he should do it?" Winford asked, meaning Stryker.

"He'll hold my leg down. You don't look strong enough, Winford. Get towels to put under my calf. I want my ankle off the table. Stryker, keep my leg from moving while he does it." June rattled off the instructions like a battlefield commander.

Winford went to the shelves, picked out two towels, and brought them to the table. After rolling the towels and placing one under June's knee and the other under her calf slightly above the ankle, he straightened, waiting for more instructions from June.

"Listen to what I tell you," June said to Winford. "Bring my legs together. Look at my right ankle. See how it's positioned. You'll need to set the left one the same. Stand at the end of the table and use both hands to grab my injured foot, one on top, and one around the heel. Gently pull it toward you, and at the same time try to twist it back into position. You may or may not hear it click or pop. You might just feel it move into place. Be firm but don't use too much force. Pull toward you first, but very slightly. All you need to do is give the ankle room to slide back in place when you push it. Then once that's done, wrap it with some kind of cloth or, better yet, a bandage if you have it, and put a board, or something similar, on each side of the ankle. Tie three belts around my foot and leg to keep the boards in place."

Winford listened intently, and then asked, "Ma'am, you want a cocaine pill?"

"No," June said. "Stryker, be firm with the leg. If you keep it pinned down, I'll be less likely to wrench my ankle while Winford tries to reset it."

Stryker had a new respect for the woman.

"Winford, after I make sure there's no infection, I'll have you make a cast for me."

"A cast? I don't believe I know what that is."

"Let's get this over with." June laid down on the table. "Stryker, press on my shin. Be firm." June closed her eyes. "All right Winford, do it."

Winford situated himself in front of June's feet. He ran his hands along both ankles, trying to get a sense of where the dislocated bones were and where they should be. "Okay, ma'am. You ready?"

June didn't answer, but Stryker saw her grip the sides of the table. "Do it," he ordered. "I don't have all day."

Wilford positioned his hands on her foot like she had told him and pulled with a gentle tug. Then he tried to work the ankle joint into its proper alignment.

June suddenly arched her back and grimaced. Stryker's powerful grip kept her leg pinned, keeping it immobile. June turned her face to the side, gritted her teeth, and stifled the urge to scream.

Stryker decided right then a woman can stand more pain than a man. *It's good thing men don't go through childbirth.*

"I'm sorry ma'am." Winford's face flushed red. Sweat beads grew to rivulets down his cheeks. "It's tough to move," he grunted. He released her heel and gripped her foot at the lateral arch. Then he pushed on the leg with more force.

June's body slackened.

"She's fainted. Get it done," Stryker growled.

"Move dammit!" Winford pulled and twisted the foot more forcefully. When he went to push, the foot slipped into place on its own. "I think I got it."

Winford used the towels to wrap around June's ankle and lower leg. He left and returned with two straight, wooden chair slats. He didn't say where he got them. Using the three belts, he fastened the slats to her leg.

"You got an extra bed?" Stryker asked.

"Well, I guess..."

The mixed breed scooped June up off the table. "Let's go."

"What's going on?" The matronly, stern-faced woman asked when Stryker, carrying June, followed Winford through the front door.

"Flora, this is, uh, Mister Stryker. His wife had dislocated her ankle."

Flora held her tongue. It was not entirely clear why. Could have been her consideration for another woman, or perhaps, she chose not to rile the man carrying the woman.

"Bring her on in. We'll put her in this other bedroom," Flora said, crossing the living room and opening the door to a small bedroom. It may have been a child's room at one time. It had a twin bed and a walnut chest with four drawers for furniture. A window with white lace curtains was opposite the bed and wall.

Stryker laid June on the bed. She'd regained consciousness in Stryker's arms, but said nothing when Winford mentioned she was Stryker's wife. June glanced at her splinted ankle on the bed, looked up at Stryker, and said, "it feels better."

"Miss June's a doctor," Winford said to his wife.

"See if she wants anything to eat," Stryker grunted to Flora. "C'mon, Winford."

"Stryker..." June called after him.

He paused and turned around.

"Thank you."

Stryker led Winford out of the house to the Gypsy wagon. "The woman's daughter is in there dead." He climbed inside and waited for Winford to follow, but the mortician wasn't tall enough to step up without help. He got no help from the mixed breed and gave up trying to climb in.

"Killed with a rock to the head. Fix her up and get her in the ground," Stryker said, bending down to gather up Sarah's body. He carried it out of the wagon, spurning Winford's offer to help. Winford dropped his arms and ran ahead to open the door. After Stryker laid the body on the same table where June had been, he pulled out a twenty-dollar note and gave it to Winford. "Take care of both women."

Stryker walked outside, untied the roan from the rear of the wagon, and rode to the stable. There, he turned his horse over to the stable boy and set off walking to the pier.

"Your husband left." That's what Winford told June when she asked about Stryker.

"He's not my husband," June said flatly. One couldn't be sure if she wished it so, or not.

"Miss?" Winford asked. "Your daughter, and your face, did he... I mean, I'm sorry about your girl's passing."

"No, he didn't beat me and kill my daughter, if that's what you're asking. Three men broke into our wagon last night. We fought them, Sarah and me, but they carried her off." Tears welled up in June's eyes. "I'm sure they had their way with her before they killed her."

"That Mister Stryker found your daughter dead and brought her back to you." Flora guessed correctly."

"He did."

"The men, they'd gone? They just left the poor girl?" Flora asked.

"No, Stryker killed them."

"He killed all three?"

"Slit their God-damned throats," June cursed. A hateful scowl darkened her face.

CHAPTER NINE

S tryker strode to the docks about as frustrated as he had ever been. The delays caused failure, an inadequacy he abhorred. Not that he gave a shit how other people felt about him, rather it was his own evaluation that annoyed him. The mission itself was no help, either. Perils of a paramour–if that's who Tami was to Hearst–hadn't been a big concern to him. Could that have been the reason he allowed his normally alert mind to wander and not be aware of the danger a log chute presented? Almost two months now, and still not back to full self. *Shit on that too.* And now, he thought. *And now, God-dammit!* An innocent girl lay dead because of him. The mother now grieves over her death. She'd saved his life, and that was how he repaid her. *You're welcome, June. Is there anything else I can do for you?* Go find this Stanek fellow and kill the son-of-a-bitch, Stryker groused to himself. At least get that right.

The 80-foot *Meteor* lay quietly moored to the dock. Early morning mist shrouded the ship, and Stryker could barely see its ghostly shape at the end of the pier. The steamship, considered to be the fastest boat of her kind in the world with a maximum speed of 30 mph, was owned by Duane Bliss, who used it as a workhorse year-round on the lake. A low-slung side wheeler, it had an iron hull, a beam of 10 feet, and was normally used to pull log booms across the lake. The *Meteor* wasn't the only steamer on the lake. Eight other steamers plied on its waters. Now days, tourist business was flourishing, and today being Saturday, a slow logging day, the haul consisted mainly of sight seekers taking a tour around the lake. Stryker bought a ticket to Incline on the *Meteor*. A half hour remained before departure, but small groups of passengers, twenty or so persons in all, stood on the pier chatting with each other. Much of the conversation centered around the chilly morning, giving the notion many of the passengers were from places of lower altitudes. The ship could carry up to eighty people comfortably, depending on the cargo load.

Another group of waiting passengers were at a wooden stand to buy mugs of hot coffee from a crewmember. The aroma wafting in the air enticed Stryker to walk over and buy a cup. It had been a while. He was tired, not wanting to talk, and he stood away from the others on the pier sipping the steaming brew. A few minutes later, he boarded the *Meteor* along with the rest of the passengers.

The fog hadn't fully lifted and the cold air blowing past him on the fast-moving steamer chilled his hand holding the coffee. About half of the passengers sought relief from the cold wind by crowding toward the stern and under cover. The more hardy remained clustered on the bow and were treated with spectacular views of the snow-capped mountains against patches of blue sky. Much of the slopes had been stripped of trees. Nevertheless, the mountains and the crystal-clear lake still afforded those who braved the cold, a stunningly beautiful picture.

Stryker was finishing the coffee when the *Meteor* slowed and swung around to dock at Incline. Fast trip, he thought, and he drained the last drops. *Now, at last, it's time to find that bastard Russian.* He placed the mug on the metal tray by the roped ramp and walked off the *Meteor* and onto the soil of Incline. "Where can I find a logger called Stanek?" He asked a trio of men wearing logger attire–wool shirt, canvas pants, and heavy boots–waiting to board the ship. He got no immediate reply, prob-ably because he didn't look like a man looking for a logging job. The menacing Colt hanging low on his hip wasn't used for shooting trees. Stryker waited, but he did not look patient. His hand drifted to the Peace-maker. One of the three men summoned a reply. "You mean the Russian.

He's over by the incline. Most days, you'll find him at the bottom or the top."

The "incline" the logger referred to was a funicular railway. Two tracks, four rails were laid 4,000 feet up the side of the mountain. Its vertical climb was 1,400 feet. Loggers loaded cut logs onto rail cars, and the cars, attached to an 8,000-foot haul line, were pulled up the mountain by the steam donkey anchored on top. The looped cable pulled loaded cars up and let empty cars down at the same time. Each trip up took about twenty minutes. On the eastern side of the mountain, logs were sent down a dry flume which wound its way to the 3,000-foot Virginia and Gold Hill water tunnel and on to the Truckee River. Then they floated to Carson City. From there, the Virginia-Truckee Line carried logs to Virginia City. Over time, as the mines played out, more logs got diverted to other towns. Back then, a store, a stable, a boardinghouse, and some cabins were all which existed in what eventually grew to become Incline Village.

Mining in Virginia City did slow considerately by the mid1880's and the demand for lumber from the Tahoe area had also diminished. However, logging continued around the lake, just not as much as in the prior decades. But men still loaded the incline cars with cut logs, though not with as many logs, and not with as many men to load them. Stryker had no trouble finding the incline. The mountain had been clear cut and the four rails were visible all the way to the top. He fell in behind an oxen team pulling logs and followed them to the turn-about at the bottom of the hill. The cable wound around a six-foot pulley-wheel. Two flatbed rail cars were permanently attached to the cable uphill from the wheel. Using a massive block and tackle system, workmen winched the heavy logs up from the ground and swung them onto the waiting cars. Once the logs were loaded and chained in place, a couple of men would hop on for the ride up the mountain. After the second car was loaded, Stryker climbed aboard. He got curious glances from the men sitting atop the logs, but nothing more. He guessed they figured he had business at the top and that business was none of theirs.

"Took a long time to find the son of a bitch," Stryker said out loud as he looked up the mountain. He sat facing uphill, but as the car took him higher, he turned briefly to take in the view of Lake Tahoe. Even without all the trees, the view was inspiring. He faced forward again. What needed his attention was on top of the hill. Ascending the mountain seemed like a metaphor for the mixed breed. He'd been climbing over one God-damned obstacle after another to get where he was now, and he was climbing up to get to finally the bottom of Tami's troubles and solve the damn mystery.

Skies were clearing now, and the sun shone brightly on the mountain. A hawk circled near the top looking for breakfast, and off to the right, three white-tailed deer scrambled away from the tracks. The two men on the car with him talked in low tones, chuckling at times over something they must have thought funny. It was a beautiful day. A good day to kill a man.

The cars slowed as they approached the crest of the mountain. Up ahead, on top, a group of loggers waited by the steam donkey, and Stryker tried to tell if one of them might be the Russian. Nope.

A windowless weather shack, the steam donkey, an outhouse, and a corral holding a few oxen and mules, stood atop the ridge. A little past the crest of the ridge on the western slope lay the start of the V-shaped logging flume. The flume like other dry flumes was greased with butter and animal fat to make the logs slide better. Several more workmen who held pikes stood by, ready to load logs for their slide to the water flume and tunnel and then on down to the railroad.

Stryker hopped off with the other two men before the car came to a complete stop. The steam donkey, clanking its pistons and drive shafts, made an awful racket, too loud for a decent conversation near the thing. Stryker walked briskly to a worker standing twenty feet away from the donkey and yelled, "Where's the Russian?" Normally he'd take his time and nose around before he made his move, get a sense of how things were, the lay of the land, etc. But Stryker was eager to conclude business.

"Where's Stanek?" Stryker shouted again. He saw a burly man emerging from the weather shack suddenly take off, running toward the flume. The fellow shoved two more loggers with pikes out of his way and jumped in the greased chute. He sat there, with his feet pointed downhill, grabbing at the top edges in a desperate attempt to start his slide. The wood, recently greased, helped propel him on his way.

Stryker broke into a sprint, but running in cowboy boots proved too awkward for a rapid dash, and the Russian was well on his way down the mountain when Stryker reached the flume.

And Stanek was picking up speed, too much speed. The slide turned into a dangerous plummet. A quarter mile down the chute, he tried to slow himself. His arms flailed wildly on the sides with his hands gathering painful splinters. Then he tried bracing himself with his boots. A slight rise in the slope or a crack in the planks wouldn't affect a heavy log. But a man sitting upright and trying to jam his boots had a different outcome. A boot found a crack at just the right moment and Stanek sailed out of the flume. Flapping his arms and bicycling his legs, he managed to "fly" twenty feet before crashing to earth. The hapless Russian rolled another ten feet and ended his journey against a tree stump on the eastern side of the Sierra Nevada's.

Alive, but dazed, Stanek hadn't fully recovered his senses when Stryker got to him. Standing over the Russian, with a drawn Peacemaker, Stryker growled, "Hello Stanek."

Stanek appeared to be somewhere between five-foot ten and six feet. It was hard to tell. He was lying on the ground. He was not fat but thick-chested under the red plaid shirt. He had angular facial bones and brushy eyebrows. His large snout was bleeding and shoved to one side above a grossly swollen mouth. He had a one-inch diagonal cut resembling a bloody hair-lip under the battered nose.

"Think my shoulder's broke," Stanek mumbled through bloody lips, and pushing himself upright. His accent was thick and coarse. He rolled to all threes and struggled to his feet with considerable effort. He stood with his back to Stryker.

Stryker holstered the Colt, pulled the sai, and stepped closer. He flipped the weapon in his hand, prongs back along his forearm, readying to drive the handle end into Stanek's forehead when he turned. He wouldn't kill him right away. He wanted answers first.

However, Stanek swung a meaty arm around behind him, hard and fast. The blow hit Stryker's cocked arm, knocking the sai aside. Stanek whirled with agility that caught the mixed breed by surprise. He hadn't expected catlike moves by the Russian's bulky body, and before he could recover, Stanek lunged.

The attack forced Stryker backward, causing him to trip over a sawed log laying on the ground behind his feet. Stryker hit the ground hard and landed on a pointed rock that sent stabbing pain shooting down his spine. He tried to roll away to keep Stanek from landing on him, but his reflexes were slowed by the numbing pain.

Stanek's shoulder must have indeed been injured, because he used only one hand to grab at Stryker's throat. One was enough. It was an iron grip and Stanek threw his full weight into it, shoving his shoulder against his hand to crush against Stryker's windpipe.

Stryker still held the sai, but he couldn't reverse it to bring the needle point prongs into play. Instead, he struck Stanek's temple with the pummel end. Again, and again, and fourth time, as he began to lose consciousness. Then the grip on his throat loosened. Stryker jammed a boot into the ground and got enough leverage to roll the dazed Russian off him.

Stryker got to his knees, dropped the sai, and pulled the Colt. Stanek lay on his back, foaming at the mouth. Stryker leaned over and rammed the gun barrel in his mouth. He cocked the hammer.

"Before I shoot your Russian ass, Tami wants to know why you tried to kill her."

Stanek tried to talk, but the gun barrel wedged against the back of his throat made him gag.

Stryker withdrew the Colt and jammed the barrel up a swollen nostril. "Talk, fucker."

"What? Not try to kill her. I love her."

Stryker wanted to kill him. He fought mightily not to pull the trigger. The man was the ultimate cause of Sarah's death. Stryker wouldn't be in Tahoe, were it not for the Russian. He wouldn't have been injured were it not for the Russian. Tami wouldn't have been burned out were it not for the Russian. *Easy, now. Hold off. Get all the answers first.*

"You love her," Stryker growled. He eased his finger off the trigger, just barely though.

"Since the day I seen her," Stanek groaned, rubbing his shoulder. The gun remained stuck up his nose. It bled from the cut made by the front sight blade.

"Russians woo women by burning down their houses?" Stryker's trigger finger grew itchy again.

"No." Stanek started to shake his head but the gun barrel lodged up his snout wouldn't let him.

"I would've shot you already, but Tami's curious. Why then?" Stryker sat back on one knee. He withdrew the Colt and aimed it between Stanek's eyes.

"Yes, shoot me. I make big mistake." Stanek tore his eyes away front the gun barrel and looked up at Stryker. "I ain't much handsome. Think Tami only want me if she has no money." Stanek shut his eyes and grimaced.

"You're not only ugly. You're stupid." And at this moment, the mixed breed decided he would try to do something good. Though, he was torn between that and killing every man on top of the mountain, he blew a long breath, and said, "You dumbass bastard. You're gonna make it up to her." He holstered the Colt. "Get on your feet."

Stryker made Stanek go ahead of him climbing up the four-hundred yards to the ridge top and the rattling steam donkey. He figured the Russian told him the truth, but why chance it? Stanek stumbled several times, and Stryker would have helped him, but a man like Stryker can only do so much good.

"These fellows all work for you?" Stryker asked, eyeing eight men piking the cut timber off rail cars. Other men were chaining logs to oxen and dragging them to the flume. Oxen are stronger than draft horses, but they are more likely to kill a man. Stryker estimated about thirty men in total labored on top with another twenty or so down below.

"Yes," Stanek nodded. "They work for me, and another forty cutting, de-limbing, and bucking. Have more than a hundred men working for me," he bragged.

"Doing well for yourself, I reckon," Stryker said, as he watched another pair of railcars crest the ridge.

"I make good living." Stanek slipped off his belt to use a sling. "I need a doctor for my shoulder."

"You'll see one in Tahoe City. Tell your men I'm taking you to the doctor."

"Men! Hurt my shoulder!" Stanek yelled to the oxen drivers. "Dax, you're in charge 'til I get back! Shouldn't be long." He glanced sideways, with arched eyebrows at Stryker. "That right, mister?"

"Depends on you." Stryker eyed the shack. "What's in there?"

"Stove, worktable, chairs, two beds. Wait there 'til cars unloaded?" Stanek asked.

"If your men try anything, you'll get the first bullet." Stryker figured no workers saw him pull the Colt on Stanek, but they probably suspected he ran for a reason. "Get in there," he said, nodding toward the shack. Stanek went inside and lay on one of the bunks, groaning on every other breath. His nose and mouth had almost stopped bleeding. Stryker sat by the door and watched the logs being unloaded. It took twenty-five minutes of the Russian's groaning for the last log to hit the ground. Stryker rose to his feet. "Let's go, Stanek."

As they rode the incline down, Stryker faced downhill and surveyed the alpine basin. Even with most of the trees cut, especially the sugar pines, the lake still glittered blue, and Stryker figured someday there would be a lot of tourists coming to see it. For now, though, he had a job to finish.

They boarded a smaller, albeit slower, side-wheel steamer with a crew of two. Stanek kept it docked at Incline for his personal use. Forty feet in length, the mahogany trimmed Spinner cut through the waves gracefully but not nearly as fast as the Meteor. The Spinner could only accommodate twelve people, but it did so comfortably with cushioned seats and curved mahogany slats for back rests. The chairs provided a much more enjoyable ride than the hard wooden benches on other larger steamers. A crew member helped Stanek board and take his seat near the rear. Stryker sat behind him and kept an eye on the two crewmen in front. It was late in the afternoon when they pulled alongside the dock at Tahoe City.

"No doctor here. We must travel to Truckee," Stanek grumbled. He made no effort to get up from his seat.

"There's a doctor here. Get up," Stryker ordered. The crewmen busied themselves, securing the boat to the dock. They evidently decided against interfering with the menacing man with a well-used gun on his hip. Maybe they didn't care all that much for their boss, either.

Stanek pushed himself to his feet, using his good arm. One of the crewmen came over to steady him, and the Russian managed to step from the rocking boat and onto the pier without falling. When they reached the end of the pier, Stryker pointed toward the dentist/mortuary house up the street, and he gave Stanek a shove in the back.

"Hey there, Stanek!" A heavily accented shout came from behind. "Where's my fifty-three dollars?"

Stryker and Stanek turned around and faced the man.

He was a big one, maybe four inches over six feet and plenty beefy. Dressed in logger's clothing, canvas pants, wool shirt, heavy boots, and a knit hat he might have had business with Stanek.

"Said I'd pay ya at the end of the month," Stanek replied gruffly.

"I want it now." The hefty logger got a better look at the mixed breed and followed with a slightly less aggressive tone. "You're here and I won't have to go to Incline for it." He then garnered more pugnacity as a man often tries after sizing up another fellow he might come to blows with. "I think you can pay me now." He took a step toward Stanek. Perhaps he thought he'd only have to handle the man who had his arm in a sling. So far, Stryker hadn't interjected himself in the dispute. He'd taken on two men at the same time before. Sometimes he came out ahead. Sometimes he didn't.

Neither Stanek nor the logger saw Stryker draw the Colt. It seemed to just appear in his hand. They did hear the hammer click, though. Cocked and pointed, the black end of the barrel looked eager to belch a .44 bullet.

The logger stared at the Peacemaker. Stanek stared at Stryker, both men awed by the speed of Stryker's draw.

"I can wait." The big man raised open palms and backed away.

Stryker motioned the gun barrel for Stanek to walk. He didn't have to do it twice. He eased the hammer forward but kept the Colt drawn.

As they got closer, Stanek saw the signs out front and stopped. He turned to Stryker with fear in his gray Slavic eyes. "Where you taking me?"

"Doctor. Keep walking."

"Three of your Russian friends beat the shit out of a whore in Truckee."

Stanek stopped and faced Stryker. "I didn't tell 'em to."

"What'd you need to know about me, Stanek?"

"You?" Now, Stanek might have suspected Tami had a lover, and that man was pointing the Peacemaker at him.

"Yeah, me." Stryker said.

Stanek eyed the gun as he spoke. "You will marry Tami?"

"No."

"She not like you?" Stanek asked. He sounded hopeful.

"Came here to kill you, not court the woman," Stryker said, matter-of-factly.

Stanek looked relieved. "I'll tell my men not to ask about you."

"No need. They're dead."

"Dead? You killed them?" Stanek asked.

Stryker motioned with the gun again and they resumed walking until they got to the front of the mortuary.

Stanek hesitated. It was clear he didn't want to walk up to the front door. Stryker persuaded him with a poke of the Colt in his back. Cocking the hammer probably helped as well. "Move it, Stanek."

Stanek took a few tentative steps, and Stryker poked him in the back again. "Doctor's inside. Knock on the door."

Flora opened the door. "You're back," she said, in a not so friendly greeting. "I see you have Stanek there with you." She glimpsed at the .44 Stryker held on the Russian. "What's he done?"

"Injured his shoulder." Stryker answered. He looked past Winford's wife and saw June sitting in the front room. She sat on a stuffed chair with her foot propped on a footstool. He prodded Stanek with the gun barrel. "Go in." Flora closed the door behind them and came around in between the men and June.

"She's feeling a little better," Flora said, giving a kindhearted smile toward June.

"Stryker." June's face was still bluish and puffy, but the swelling had gone down a little. Her hair had been combed and tied in the back. She seemed pleased to see the mixed breed; however, the woman looked drained. The tears were dried now and although the woman couldn't muster a smile, there was a slight crinkling around the eyes. "I didn't expect to see you again so soon." She kept her eyes on Stryker, ignoring Flora and Stanek, and even Wilford who came into the room from the rear.

"Good to see you up a bit. How you doing, doctor?" Stryker addressed June by her profession for Stanek's benefit. He holstered the Colt.

"All right." June said. I'm trying to cope. "But the problem with death is that it is *so* final."

Stryker nodded grimly. "Nothing's more final."

"Thankfully, my ankle wasn't broken, just out of place." June changed the subject. She sat up in the chair.

"Stryker," Wilford offered his own greeting. "We've had a long talk while you were away."

Stryker reluctantly shifted his attention from June to Wilford. Stryker said nothing, figuring the mortician had more to say.

"Uh well..." Wilford, began with some hesitation, seemingly caught off guard by Stryker's silence. "Sarah will be interned here in Tahoe City. A memorial will be erected for her by the lake. June will stay here too, to be close by." Wilford looked at June with a kindly smile. "We'll need a good doctor here, what with all the tourists coming to Lake Tahoe," he added, brightening the mood.

"Here's your first patient," Stryker said, hooking a thumb at Stanek. "Hurt his shoulder."

Stanek stared at June, gingerly holding his arm. He looked kinda doubtful.

"Come over here and let me see your shoulder." June dropped her foot off the stool and scooted it aside with her hand. Stryker gave Stanek a push. He stumbled forward to stand in front of June.

"Bend down." June leaned forward and gently felt around Stanek's arm, shoulder, and clavicle. He winced as she inspected the injury, but didn't cry out. "How did you hurt it?" June released his arm and sat back.

"I fell out a log flume and landed on it pretty hard."

June glanced at Stryker and then back to Stanek, who'd straightened. "Well, Stanek, your shoulder's dislocated. Are you in much pain?"

"It hurts," Stanek said, cradling his forearm.

"I can fix it, but it'll hurt more as I do it," June warned. "Just need to close the reduction a little."

"Huh?" Stanek backed up two steps.

Stryker placed a hand on the hesitant Russian's back and shoved him forward. "Fix it, June," Stryker said, forgetting to call her "doctor."

"All right Stanek, bend down here again." June lifted her arms toward the Russian. "Let your arm hang straight and keep it straight."

June gripped his upper arm in one hand and his shoulder with the other, and began gentle manipulation. Stanek's face contorted in pain as she worked the arm back in its socket. June dropped her hands beside her and sat back on the cushion. Lifting her injured foot, she used her good leg to maneuver the stool back under her ankle. "It's done. Keep a sling on for a couple of days and don't use your arm. After that, gradually increase range of motion, but don't lift or push anything for a while. Important you don't keep it immobile too long. It could freeze up on you. How does it feel now?"

Stanek raised up, rubbing his shoulder. A big smile erupted on his face. "It don't hurt."

"Pay her, Stanek. Ten dollars oughta cover it," Stryker said.

Using his uninjured arm, Stanek dug out a fistful of coin from his pocket. He held out his palm to June, and she picked out a ten-dollar gold piece.

Stryker tipped his Stetson. "Thanks, doctor." Then turning to the Russian, "C'mon Stanek, you've got business in Truckee."

June watched Stryker escort Stanek out the front door. Hard to tell what she was thinking as she watched Stryker leave.

Stryker and Stanek walked directly to the Tahoe City stable. While there to pick up the roan, Stryker ordered Stanek to rent a horse, a bay mare, for three dollars a day. They rode out of Tahoe City side by side, heading northwest along the river to Truckee. It was close to seven o'clock, but still fairly light, when the two men rode into Truckee.

"Will you tell me what we will do here?" Stanek asked, as they rode the horses at a slow walk down Donner Pass Road. He had to shout the question because the saloons they rode past were already full of loud drunks.

"Keep going to the Whitney Hotel. Rein left on Bridge Street." Stryker nodded straight ahead. Stanek failed to see the Stetson dip, but he kept the mare walking east toward the hotel.

"Are we meeting someone there?"

"Tahoe Tami."

Out of the corner of his eye Stryker saw Stanek arch his back and stick out his chest. He rode taller in the saddle. The shops had shuttered their doors, and most of the men in the street were inebriated loggers going from one watering hole to another. They rode up to the front entrance of the Whitney Hotel and tied the roan and mare to the rail posts. Stryker didn't have to prod Stanek to enter. In fact, Stryker noticed a jauntiness in the Russian's steps as he climbed the wooden planks to the front doors. *Infatuation, love, or lust, makes a man do funny things,* Stryker mused to himself.

Inside the hotel, kerosine wall lamps supplemented fading sunlight. Still, light from the lanterns merely poked holes in the dimly lit lobby. After asking the front desk of Tami's whereabouts, Stryker led Stanek into the dining room. The dining room had two windows which helped brighten its interior, even with the sun sinking behind mountains to the west. They found Tami eating supper. Seated at a small circular table in a dim corner, she was engaged in an intense conversation with Dud. Neither of them noticed Stryker and Stanek enter the dining room. Stanek followed timidly behind Stryker.

"Hello, Tami," Stryker said, interrupting Dud and Tami. He made no move to draw up chairs for him or Stanek.

Tami suddenly jerked about and seemed genuinely excited to see the mixed breed. "Stryker!"

"This is the fellow burning down your taverns." Stryker announced, grabbing Stanek by the collar and pulling Stanek up beside him.

Tami swung her attention to Stanek. "Him?"

"Says he loves you." Stryker replied dryly.

Stanek shuffled his feet, and after awkwardly studying his boots for an absurdly long time, he stared over Tami's head with a stupid look on his face.

Tami eyed Stanek with suspicion. "Excuse me?"

Before Stanek could mine the words from a stupefied brain, Stryker answered for him. "In Russia, to properly woo a woman, you burn down her house." Stryker couldn't resist.

"You wha–?" Tami tore her eyes from the pitiful-looking Russian and turned back to the mixed breed. "Burn down my...?

"All right," Stryker clarified. "He thought if you had no money and were desperate, you might be open to his courtin'."

"Well, for God's sake," Tami exclaimed, obviously quite dismayed.

"To make it up to you..." Stryker began. "He's gonna build you the most fabulous, magnificent saloon in Truckee, aren't you, Stanek?"

Stankek's face brightened. "Yes ma'am, I will." He doffed his knit cap and nervously rotated it in his large burly hands. He offered Tami a big smile and then it slinked off his face.

"I think someone wants to speak to you, Stryker," Tami said, looking past him.

"Please excuse me for the intrusion," said the hotel clerk, looking somewhat uncomfortable. He'd come up behind Stryker and Stanek without being seen, except by Tami. "Mister Stryker, sir, you have a person waiting in your room," he announced apologetically."

"Tell him where you want the tavern and he'll buy the land." Stryker said to Tami, ignoring the clerk. "He'll build it to your specifications, so draw up what you want."

"That right?" Tami sounded incredulous.

"Yes, ma'am. You just tell me," Stanek beamed. Could be he was motivated by more than just pure love. Perhaps Stryker's Peacemaker provided additional motivation. Regardless, even a bullet took a back seat to the love of his life. He glanced at Dud.

Dud nodded in agreement. "She'd be mighty grateful."

"If you don't do it, Stanek, I'll be back," Stryker growled. "Wouldn't mind seeing that doctor again." Stryker added the June comment for two reasons. He wanted Stanek to know he would return, and second, he really wouldn't mind seeing her again.

As Stryker walked from the dining room, he heard Tami say to Stanek, "You're not all that ugly. Gotta fix that nose, though."

Who the hell could be in his room? Stryker left the dining room, crossed the lobby, and started up the stairs. He drew the Peacemaker. When he reached the third floor, he stepped lightly down the hall toward room *312*. It seemed as if it'd been a month instead of just one day. All but one of the hall lanterns was out and he ran his left hand along the wall, counting six doors to his room. He flattened against the wall. No light showed underneath the door.

Stryker thumbed the hammer on the Colt and leveled it at the door. He stretched out his hand, turned the doorknob, and the kicked the door open. Nothing.

He peeked inside. A candle burned on the desk. *A candle?* It hardly threw off any light.

"You comin' in, or are you gonna stay out there all night? It was a female voice

"Morgan." Stryker recognized her. He holstered the Peacemaker and entered the room.

"We got no word for almost two months, other than what the two half-breed girls told us," Morgan sat reclined on the bed, blanket up to her neck.

Stryker reached for the desk lantern.

"Don't light it," Morgan said. "You could have let us know something."

"Had an accident. Been trying to be good." Even in the dim candle light he could see her prominent cheekbones. She looked damn good.

"Good? As in a good man?"

"Yes."

"I don't want a 'good' man. If I wanted a 'good' man, I'd get myself a sanctimonious preacher. I want the man who has 'Evil' on his saddle." She threw off the blanket, revealing she was fully naked. "Now, get over here and nail my ass to the bed."

Stryker picked up the candle and sat beside Morgan. She lay back on the bed. Holding the flame by her face, he was reminded why he always thought her attractive. Her hair was straight and parted on one side, eyes dark and piercingly intelligent, delicate facial bones above slightly hollow cheeks. And those lips, full, but not puffy, were delectably soft and yielding. He leaned down to taste them.

He sat up and held the candle over the soft skin of her belly, tilting it so that a drop of hot wax poured out and dripped on her.

"Oh!" Morgan flinched, sucking in a sharp breath.

He tipped the candle again, making a tiny puddle in her navel. Morgan didn't flinch this time. And he dripped more past her navel, marching little drops of hot wax down to her pubic mound, and then one last drop below that.

"You really are a devil, Stryker," Morgan whispered.

He blew out the candle, undressed, and stretched out beside her. Propped up on one elbow, he stroked her hair. Leaning closer, he lightly kissed her forehead.

"You've lost weight," she said, feeling along his ribs. "What happened?"

"Log hit me. Think about something else."

Morgan closed her eyes. What was it about this man? Why was he different? Her husband, when they were first married, was a good lover, certainly a good husband and father to their son. But even during the best of lovemaking–and she thought her husband *was* the best before he got so engrossed in his work–he was nothing like Stryker. *Couldn't hold a candle.* She cracked a grin, thinking about the candle. So, what was it? Stryker wasn't what many women would call handsome, and some would even say he's ugly because of his fierce countenance. *He's a killer,* she thought. *A heartless, ruthless killer.* She'd seen him kill, although sometimes on her behalf, but he did it so proficiently, so callously. The gun looked natural in his hand, not awkward like in a lot of men's hands. For him, it was just a handy tool for killing, like the razor, and that evil-looking sai he carried. The thought of him using those weapons on someone caused her body to shudder. She wondered if Stryker thought it was because of his touch.

Good God, she thought. *Is that the reason?* She's attracted to him *because* he's a ruthless killer. Was that it? That he possessed the power and the skills to kill a man? Was it the killer hands caressing her now making her feel this way? Was that what brought her such pleasure? *My God, what kind of person am I?*

Was she special to him? Was it that he became a different man around her? Thoughtful? Considerate? Maybe, could be. *I hope so.* Stryker's fingers which had been gently toying with her nipples, moved down her body to softly caress a swollen clitoris, and she laid her ruminations aside.

Stryker felt inside. She was wet, very wet. He withdrew his fingers and used his tongue to moisten the tips. And then he began to draw little circles around her clitoris. A gasp escaped her lips. Her fingers found his erect penis, and she spread pre-seminal fluid around the head of his erection. The tips of her fingers, delicate and feminine made the rigid member involuntarily twitch.

Time to get to work, Stryker decided.

He moved on top with little effort. Morgan thoughtfully helped with a guiding hand, and he slipped inside. Slow at first, letting her get used to the size of him, then harder and deeper. Holding it in deep, circling and grinding. He raised his body up and brought her hand down to her clitoris. She tried to pull away, and he grabbed her wrist, commanding she pleasure herself while he rose and fell against her. He could feel her hand working her clitoris when he was in deep. It was all he could do to hold off. She used her other hand on his rear, urging him to drive back in each time he rose. After several long minutes, he placed his hands under her buttocks and canted her hips for even deeper plunging. Many deep thrusts later, he withdrew his hand and bit it, concentrating on the pain, fighting the urge to come. It had been a while but the urge subsided.

Pumping harder now, and Morgan was emitting little grunts with each thrust.

A deep guttural growl started way down inside her and rose to escape in a one long sensual grunt. She pulled her hand from underneath and wrapped her arms tightly around his back, trying to immobilize him while she enjoyed an elongated orgasm.

Stryker brought her to four more. He could tell she had to work hard on the fifth one, and he opted to concentrate on his own release. It started in his lower spine, tingled his testicles, and then he spurted a gusher. Ten more minutes of good hard fucking, and he had another. No way he could match five, though. He rolled off.

"Surprised you came," Stryker said, catching his breath, resting on his back.

"Five of 'em," Morgan said.

NOTES

CHAPTER 1

1. See Book 5, *Christmas Slay*
2. See Book 5 "Christmas Slay

CHAPTER 3

1. See *Left to Die*, Book 1 in the Evil Stryker Series

Not Today

"Two hundred feet down, that ought to do it." He perched on the granite precipice, his feet dangling over the edge. Looking down between the Hyer Western Boots, he could see an apron of large, jagged boulders spreading out from the base of the cliff. The landing would be messy. A strong wind swept up from below and blew hard against his face, causing the man to squint his pale gray eyes slivers of steel. The long black hair, which normally touched the shoulders, waved out behind his head. He leaned back.

Farther away from the cliff, a stream meandered through the meadow on its path to a small lake off to its right. On the far side of the meadow, a stand of blue tip spruce with sprinkles of quaking aspens stretched out to the opposite cliff. Together, the trees and the cliff on which he sat collared the scenic valley. A group of five white tail deer munched in the lush grass below, and a bald eagle circled lazily over the lake, looking for breakfast. Two adult marmots with two smaller young ones scurried from the boulders. They disappeared in berry bushes by the stream. Creatures in nature, all busy with active lives, were oblivious to the man on the rock about to end his.

The night before, in a town called Whisper, he'd eaten and drank in Drake's, the town's only saloon. He ate sparingly. He drank heavily.

Starting with beer and then switching to whiskey, because he wasn't getting drunk quickly enough, he almost drowned the memories. But not quite.

He is a tall man, six feet-three and weighing just over two hundred pounds. He could pour a good amount of liquor down him when he felt like it. That didn't happen all that much. However, it did last night. The dream the prior night was a bad one. They'd been coming more often now, invading his sleep at night. It'd sometimes take all day to purge them out of his mind during the day. He hated them. He hated them because they always had him killing his wife. He'd been careless. The artillery round had landed out of sector; another man put the wrong coordinates on the howitzer. He should have checked them though. As the officer in charge of the firing demonstration, it had been his job to do that. Her body lay shattered, bleeding, and blackened due to the shell's explosion. He ran to her lying on the ground, and she still lived–for a few precious moments. Bubbling from her lips in blood before she died, she'd said his name, "Stryker."

And then there was the guilt. It weighed on his shoulders like a heavy yoke.

Leigh was her name. They had happy times, good times. He hadn't known them before her or since. Before, he couldn't dodge the shit which always came his way. After her, he figured he deserved it. His attitude didn't help. He could be a real prick, and he knew it. He didn't care. Nice wasn't in him. It hightailed out of Stryker a long time ago to find a better home. His features sure didn't hide the kind of man he was. His eyes were like those of a predator bird, cold and pale. He had hollow cheeks with a week-old beard along a firm jaw, and a mustache that drooped at the ends, Mexican style. His countenance suggested him capable of immense cruelty. He was.

Guilt was the only thing that cut the grief. Shit.

Last night at Drake's saloon, Fran, a decent looking bar maid, had offered her charms, for five dollars, but he wasn't in the mood. Not that he never consorted with soiled doves. He did; so, what. He exercised his loins. The women probably didn't care for him, but they did care for the money, and they made love to the money. Fair trade.

He'd unsaddled the big roan horse, pulled bridle and bit, and let it loose. It stayed close by and munched quietly on Sierra wild rye grass, not far from Stryker. The gun belt and holster hung around the saddle horn of the United States Army saddle lying next to a ponderosa pine. The .44 Peacemaker rested in its holster. It would have been too easy, too quick. He needed to feel the last few seconds. He deserved that too.

The wind— he'd have to leap out a way to get away from the wall. He scooted back from the edge and rose to his feet. Still facing the cliff's edge, he backed up for a running jump. He hesitated for just a brief moment, gathering himself, but he only took one step before the lasso sailed over his head and settled around his torso. The lariat tightened quickly, pinning his arms to his sides. Then a strong pull of the rope jerked him off his feet. The horse and rider dragged him at a gallop over rocks and through briar bushes, slamming his body against logs and stumps before he would pop free. He fought to slip from the rope, but it was too tight. All he could do was try to roll and dodge the stumps and boulders. Finally, the horse slowed. Cut, bleeding, and badly bruised, he barely remained conscious until the dragging stopped all together. It had lasted twenty minutes.

"Is he dead?" a female asked.

"I don't think so," a male replied.

Their voices sounded far away to Stryker who lay motionless on the ground, listening.

"What're you gonna do with him Ronnie? Why'd you brung him here?" The woman sounded nervous.

"Let's get him in there with Dixie." Ronnie pulled the rope from the saddle horn, coiling it around his shoulder as he quick-stepped over to Stryker. He then unwound the rope and looped it several times around Stryker's chest and arms as he rolled the dazed, semi-conscious man. He double tied the ends. "All right lift his feet." Together, they half carried, half dragged Stryker into a broken down, two-room cabin. With numerous gaps in the rough-hewn logs and missing wooden slats on the roof, it sorely needed a craftsman's attention. Inside, an eating table still stood on four legs, but two of the four chairs around it had broken legs. Two bunks with straw matting fit in a corner. They put him in the second room, a bed room. It had a bed anyway, no other furniture. On the brass bed laid an old man with a white river of a beard stretching down his chest. He had on a well-worn, unwashed plaid shirt, and ragged denim trousers with suspenders. Dixie also had a bullet hole in the middle of his wrinkled forehead.

They propped Stryker against the foot of the bed. After the door closed, he tried reaching for the straight razor he kept in his rear pocket. He managed to work a hand to his back. The razor was still there.

"Now what?" the woman demanded in the next room. She had dirty blond hair a comb would get stuck in. Her faded blue dress hung loosely on a thin frame. Cheekbones poked out from a pallid face. She looked to be around forty. She was twenty-eight.

"Don't you go gettin' all squirrely on me Ronda. You was the one who was after me to plug ole Dixie! Ya tolt me you just couldn't go on livin' with 'im. Remember? How the hell did ya marry up with the bastard in the fust place, Rhonda? God almighty. He's older'n shit." Ronnie stood a solid six-foot in height, had an unruly mop of brown hair, and dressed his part, like a cowboy. Not as old as Rhonda at twenty-four, he was clean shaven because he still couldn't grow a beard.

"Got me outta that fuckin' swamp. You already knowed that. I done told you a hunnert times. Don't ask me no more, Ronnie. I did what I had to. Now what about that man?"

"Well, who do ya supposin' they gonna think put that hole in Dixie's head? You? And I shore ain't ownin' up to it."

Rhonda cracked a wide grin, "Him! We gonna kill him?"

"I ain't figured that part out yet. If we do, then who'd we say, did it? If we don't, we could say we caught him after he shot Dixie. He'd say he didn't do it but thar'd be two of us agin him. He was lookin' to rob you-uns. I come along. An' I beat hell outta 'im."

"I think you should shoot him. He was gonna jump anyway."

"I'm thinkin'."

"God almighty Ronnie! Shoot him. You came in on us. He killed Dixie an' was tryin' to rape me, an' you shot him for Christ sake!"

Ronnie grinned big, "Yeah, that's what happened, ain't it?

The young cowboy pulled the Navy Colt from his holster, stepped across the room, and opened the door. "Hey, wher'd he . . . aahhh!

The sharp thrust of a boot came from behind the door, kicking Ronnie's gun hand aside, and spinning his body. Ronnie now had his back to Stryker who sprang forward. Lifting the cowboy's chin, Stryker ran the razor ear to ear. It all happened in less than a second. Stryker stepped back, and Ronnie staggered into the room with Rhonda. His throat gaped open in macabre crimson laugh, spraying blood. Ronnie tried to say something but coughed and spit blood instead. He stretched out his arms toward her, but she shrank away in horror. Her lover took one more uneasy step and fell to his knees. From there he teetered for three long seconds before collapsing on the floor. A small red lake spread out next to his face.

Stryker appeared in the bedroom doorway. He paid no attention to Ronnie's death throes on the floor. He paused briefly and then walked across the floor, holding the razor still dripping blood by his side.

"You killed him?" Rhonda backed away, but Stryker was on her quickly.

He gripped her by the throat and pushed her against the opposite wall. Stryker leaned in closer, putting his face inches from Rhonda's, his ghostly pale eyes boring into hers.

She started to struggle but then let her hands drop to her sides. "You don't have to hurt me to rape me."

He brought the razor up beneath his thumb on her neck, and dug in the point. Slowly, he drew the blade across her throat, and Ronda only became aware of the cut when Stryker stepped back. He cracked open his lips in a snarl, revealing a glint of teeth. Her eyes grew wide with fright, or maybe, just maybe, she realized her life was coming to a close. "God help . . ." Rhonda's voice failed, and she could only manage a feeble whisper as her last words. Then she began to gag. Her back against the wall, she slid to the floor, and Rhonda stared at Ronnie's body, coughing twice before she died.

Stryker rode Ronnie's horse back to the cliff. The roan evidently decided munching on the grass more important than following the ruckus. It'd stayed there. Stryker buckled on the gun belt and saddled the horse. The words on his saddle skirt once read, "*MAJOR NEVILLE STRYKER*." But the elements and hard riding had worn off some of the letters, and the lovers had met up with the man now known as, "*EVIL STRYKER*."

Stryker swung onto the roan and wheeled it around to start back on the trail to Whisper. *Wonder if Fran is still charging five dollars.*

Wes Rand

ACKNOWLEDGMENTS

Thanks to my dear wife, Pamela Mitchell and my very capable editor, Stacey Smekofske

ABOUT WES RAND

Wes Rand was an Artillery Officer in the U.S. Army during the 1960s. He pays alimony. He doesn't like to golf but lives on a golf course. He has been bucked off a horse and two women.

He has a cabin in the mountains where he writes and hikes while his wife plays golf in Las Vegas. Wes enjoys living under the open skies in Nevada and Utah.

 facebook.com/wes.rand.14
instagram.com/rand.wes

www.ingramcontent.com/pod-product-compliance
Lightning Source LLC
Chambersburg PA
CBHW021332190726
48288CB00003B/1078